The Marine's Kiss

★ ★ ★

Shirley Jump

THORNDIKE
CHIVERS

This Large Print edition is published by Thorndike Press®, Waterville, Maine USA and by BBC Audiobooks Ltd, Bath, England.

Published in 2006 in the U.S. by arrangement with Harlequin Books S.A.

Published in 2006 in the U.K. by arrangement with Harlequin Enterprises II B.V.

U.S. Hardcover 0-7862-8270-3 (Romance)
U.K. Hardcover 1-4056-3677-7 (Chivers Large Print)
U.K. Softcover 1-4056-3678-5 (Camden Large Print)

The text of this Large Print edition is unabridged.
Other aspects of the book may vary from the original edition.

Set in 16 pt. Plantin by Elena Picard.

Printed in the United States on permanent paper.

British Library Cataloguing-in-Publication Data available

Library of Congress Cataloging-in-Publication Data

Kawa-Jump, Shirley.
    The marine's kiss / by Shirley Jump.
      p. cm. — (Thorndike Press large print romance)
    ISBN 0-7862-8270-3 (lg. print : hc : alk. paper)
    1. Women teachers — Fiction. 2. Marines — Fiction.
3. Large type books. I. Title. II. Thorndike Press large print romance series.
PS3611.A87M37 2006
813'.6—dc22   2005027899

To all the men and women who serve our country with honor, giving their lives to protect the freedom we all cherish. And especially to my father and husband, two military heroes who make me proud every day.

Should I or shouldn't I get involved with U.S. Marine — and homegrown hero — Nathaniel Dole?

PROS

Gorgeous!

Sexy!

He makes my heart beat superfast whenever he's around

Loves children

Didn't make fun of me for kissing a pig . . . will I _ever_ live that incident down?

Stood up for me at school in front of administration — he _is_ a hero!

Loves his family — and they live here, too

CONS

Keeps his feelings hidden . . . then again, so do I, sort of . . .

Can't tell how he feels about me, but I think he really likes me

I'm afraid he'll break my heart when he leaves again . . .

Chapter One

★ ★ ★

The pig refused to cooperate, creating a problem bigger than Green Acres and Big Valley put together. Jenny Wright needed to kiss this piece of pork in the next two and a half minutes so she could usher her third-graders back inside — before the principal caught her necking with a mammal on the school lawn on a Friday afternoon.

Dr. Margaret Davis was from the old school and didn't think Jenny's rewards program for her students' achievements did much more than waste time. Everyone in town knew the principal was hoping to be appointed superintendent next year, so she'd been cracking down on anything that made her — or her school — look bad. Jenny doubted Dr. Davis would like the pig much.

Heck, even *she* didn't like it much right now, and she'd hired it to be her pucker partner.

"Come on over here, Reginald," she whispered to the rotund pink animal. "One quick kiss and then you can go back to the farm. Nice bowl of slop waiting for you, I hear."

Reginald grunted, plopping down onto the new spring grass. He heaved a sigh and closed his eyes.

The circle of third-graders around Jenny began to laugh at the recalcitrant swine. Kissing a pig as a challenge to the kids to read one hundred books before the end of spring term had sounded like a great idea two and a half months ago, when Reginald was wallowing on a farm far away. But now that the pot-bellied three-hundred-pound beast was actually here, he didn't look very appealing.

She'd never be able to eat bacon again, that was for sure.

"Go on, Miss Wright, kiss him!" Jimmy said.

"Kiss the pig! Kiss the pig!" The chant spread through the twenty-five kids like a verbal wave. The April breeze carried it across the school lawn, into the open windows, bringing a few heads out to see what was happening.

She'd made a promise and she'd stick to it. If there was one thing Jenny Wright did, it was keep her promises. Especially to her students.

She tamped down the wave of nausea in her stomach, then came around to Reginald's face, got down on her knees in her black capris and, before she could think about what she was about to do, pressed her lips to Reginald's velvety snout.

He snarled, jerked awake and backed up quickly. Then he let out a squeal and dashed toward the bright pink "Animals Where You Want 'Em" truck. His handler, Ed Spangler, a tall man in overalls and a straw hat, laughed and helped Reginald up the ramp and into the back of the truck. He shut the door, then circled to the front. "Old Reginald hasn't moved that fast in ten years. Must be one heck of a pucker you got there."

"Gee, thanks. I think." Jenny dug her check out of her pocket. "Here you go."

"Oh, no need to pay me, ma'am. I haven't laughed that much in ages. Plus, the paper got a snapshot of your date with Reginald. I'd say that free publicity makes us about even." Ed gestured toward a young man holding a camera and standing across the street. "I thought this might make a good story, so I called the *Mercy Daily News* myself." He thumbed the strap of his overalls and nodded.

"This is going to be in the *paper?*" Oh

Lord, her career was over. Might as well start scouring the Help Wanted section now. If there was anything Dr. Davis disliked more than Jenny's unconventional teaching methods, it was *publicity* about Jenny's teaching methods.

A tension headache began to pound in her temples. She pressed her hands to her head, then tucked her hair behind her ears. She would deal with this later. Preferably after a lot of Tylenol and a huge platter of nachos.

Stuffing the check back into her pocket, she spun on her heel and flapped her arms at her class like a mother goose. "Come on, children, back inside."

"Miss Wright, what'd the pig taste like?" Jimmy Brooks asked.

"Yeah, was he all boogers and slime?" Alex Herman had a fascination with all things nasal. He'd even fashioned a nose for his clay project in art class.

"Eww, Alex. That is so gross." Lindsay Williams made a face and took a step away from him. "Miss Wright wouldn't *really* kiss a slimy pig anyway. She has taste."

"In what?"

Lindsay shrugged. "I dunno. In animals, I guess."

Not in men, Jenny thought. As far as

love lives went, she'd be willing to bet Reginald had better luck than she did. Finding a man wasn't high on her priority list right now anyway, not while she was so consumed with her class. All relationships did was complicate her life. Jenny had had enough complications to last her until she was eighty.

"Okay, that's enough. We need to get back to work." Jenny pulled open the outside door to her classroom and led the children inside. They took their seats, amid a steady stream of pig chatter and chair squeaking. Then she moved to the front of the room and clapped her hands. After a moment, the children quieted down and faced her. As always, a small thrill of triumph ran through her when her class ran like clockwork. To Jenny, a civilized and orderly class proved she was doing a good job. "Now, you all have done a wonderful job on the first level of the reading challenge. But, we still have a ways to go."

The class let out a collective groan.

"I'm willing to make it fun," Jenny said. "If you're willing to put in the work."

"Are you going to dye your hair green this time? I really liked the pink," Jimmy piped up.

"Uh, no. Not this time," Jenny said. Dr.

13

Davis had nearly gone into cardiac arrest when she'd seen the fuchsia hair Jenny had sported as a first-quarter class incentive.

"How about making us another giant ice cream sundae?" Lindsay rubbed her belly. "I didn't eat dinner at all that day."

Lindsay's mother hadn't been happy about that either. She'd called Dr. Davis to complain, resulting in another black mark on Jenny's teaching record. "Er, no, no sundaes."

"Well, what then?" the class asked.

Jenny put on a bright, work-with-me smile. "We could read just for the fun of it!"

"Nah. That's boring," Jimmy said. "We want a prize." Twenty-five nine-year-old heads nodded in agreement.

She'd created a monster. The children now expected *rewards* for making their class goals.

Maybe Dr. Davis had a point.

No, she refused to entertain that idea. Her third-graders needed every boost they could get to raise their reading level. This past winter, Mercy Elementary's scores in the state achievement tests had come back at their lowest levels in years and the school had been placed on probation. Losing their accreditation was a very real possibility, if something didn't happen. Jenny couldn't change every class, but she could darn well change her own.

In the last few years, her class had become her main priority in life. It wasn't that she'd set out to become the stereotypical spinster elementary school teacher. It had just happened that way, after too many failed relationships and one broken heart that refused to heal. And it was a heck of a lot easier to concentrate on the children than on why Jenny attracted bad dates like steel filings to a magnet.

"I'll think of something," she said, rubbing at her temples again and returning her thoughts to the class. As long as it didn't involve pigs or hair dye, she figured she'd be fine.

"Miss Wright?" the school secretary blurted over the loudspeaker. "Can you come down to the principal's office please? I'll have Miss Rhodes cover your class."

"I'll be right there," Jenny said.

Jimmy mouthed "Uh-oh." The other kids' eyes got wide. They knew that even for an adult, an impromptu trip to the principal's office meant only one thing — big trouble.

Debbie Rhodes opened the connecting door between the two third-grade classrooms and gave Jenny a sympathetic smile. "Do you think she saw the pig?" she whispered.

"How could she not? He weighed three hundred pounds and arrived in a hot-pink truck." Jenny sighed. "Guess I better go down there and face the wrath of Davis, huh?"

Debbie gave her arm a squeeze. "Good luck."

If she could have trudged in two-inch pumps, Jenny would have. It was a bit hard to look as if she was going to her execution dressed in black capris and a white sweater set. So she held her head high, straightened her shoulders and figured if she was going to get fired, she'd go out looking good.

"Dr. Davis would like to see you in her office. She said to shut the door." Bonnie, the school secretary, gave her a sad smile, as if she knew Jenny was going to enter the lair of the lion and come out like a shredded sock.

Jenny's spine slumped a little. "Okay." She crossed to the principal's office, entered the room, then closed the door behind her.

Dr. Davis sat at her desk, all business and primness. Her gray hair was woven into a tight bun, her brown checked suit perfectly pressed. She had on dark framed glasses, a chain dangling from both sides of the lenses. Dr. Davis left nothing to chance — not even losing her glasses.

"Sit down, Miss Wright." Dr. Davis didn't bother to look up from her paperwork. "I hear you had a visitor today."

"Uh, yeah. A really cute pig." Jenny pasted on her bright smile again. "The kids loved him."

"It was a distraction from their learning."

The smile fell a little. "It was a reward for reading a hundred books this term."

Dr. Davis raised her head. She dropped her glasses to her chest. "Your class read a hundred books?"

"Yes, they did." Jenny nodded. "They tried some authors for the first time. Even Jimmy Brooks read three and he didn't read at all before the pig incentive."

Dr. Davis leaned back in her chair. "You know the school has been placed on probation because of our achievement test scores this year."

"Yes, I'm aware of that."

Dr. Davis tapped at her lip with her pen, thinking. "We don't have much time to bring up our scores if we want to make a difference. You have mentioned to me, several times, that you'd like more support for your program."

"I do," Jenny said. "I really think it could work. The children have responded well to incentives and fun."

"Be that as it may, I'm not entirely sold on your methods thus far. However, I do have to worry about our accreditation. There's a grant available to the third-grade class that can demonstrate the best growth in reading skills over the school year. It can be used to buy books, computer equipment, whatever you want. I'm quite impressed with what the other teachers are accomplishing using traditional methods. . . ."

Oh, no, here it came. She was going to be stuffed back into the plain reading, writing and arithmetic box. No pink hair, no pigs. Nothing fun.

"However, you have done something unusual and had some success," Dr. Davis said, almost gritting the words out between her teeth. "Time will tell if it will pay off in test scores, but at this point, I'm ready to try almost anything. Your classroom could use that grant and our school needs to retain its accreditation. If we can raise our status, it also makes us eligible for additional state funding. A winning solution for everyone." Dr. Davis pursed her lips, then released them. "So, with all that in mind . . . you have my permission to continue with your students."

Jenny blinked. "I do?"

"Yes, but —" Dr. Davis held up a finger. "I don't want any more animals on the school lawn. No giant desserts in the art room. No painted hair. Instead, I have come up with your next reward." She gave Jenny a smile that seemed an awful lot like a lion opening his jaws.

Oh, Lord.

"Children like heroes," she continued. "And we have a local hero who has returned to town." The smile widened. "Nathaniel Dole."

"N-N-Nate?" Nate was back? He must be on leave. Since when? And why hadn't she known?

Because the days when he'd pick up the phone and call her to say he was coming home had passed a long time ago. And yet, a part of her still leaped at the thought of him returning, like some Pavlovian response to his presence.

"Is there something wrong with him?" Dr. Davis asked.

"No, no, not at all," Jenny said, shaking her head. A little too hard because her hair came out from behind her ears and whipped at her eyes.

I used to be in love with him, but that's not a problem.

Anymore.

Besides, she was twenty-nine now. All grown up. It had been, what, ten years since she'd seen him last?

Nine years and three months, whispered the little part of her brain that kept track of those kinds of things.

"Good. I think Mr. Dole would be perfect to come in and work with the kids. He's home on indefinite leave, doesn't have much to occupy his days right now and he loves children. Think of him as a sort of free aide." Dr. Davis leaned forward in her chair and slid a paper across the desk. "Here's his contact information. I'm sure with all those nine-year-olds, you could always use a helping hand."

The principal *had* found a box for Jenny. One she couldn't escape. Not only did she gain tacit approval for her teaching methods, but also a helper for the busy class.

Nate. The one man she'd vowed never to see again. As if by keeping him out of sight, she could blight him from her heart. If the plan had involved *anyone* but Nate . . .

"Oh yes, this is going to be wonderful," Jenny said. Almost as good as kissing the pig.

Nate Dole's mother had been at it again. No one else would have left a newspaper on his front stoop, with a tin of cookies to boot. He loved her for trying, but he wasn't ready to come out of his self-imposed cave. Not yet. Maybe not ever.

He'd bought the small ranch house he was living in now six years ago as a rental property investment. It had been vacant for a few weeks — good timing for a man who'd needed a cave.

Nate had told his family he was on an extended leave and needed some time alone to rest. They'd believed the extended-leave story because he'd barely been home in years. He'd always been too busy fighting the bad guys to stop off in Mercy for some R and R. He'd lied to his family, but it was a lie that bought him a little space and some time to figure out the rest of his life. Or what was left of it now that he was down a knee.

He turned and hobbled back into the house, using the despicable cane to help keep the weight off his left leg. It made him feel ninety, not twenty-nine, and the minute he could get around without it, he was going to use it to start a bonfire.

When he'd shut the door, he reached for the cookies and pried off the lid. He paused, a chocolate chip cookie halfway to his mouth, and noticed the picture on the front page of the Sunday edition of the *Mercy Daily News.*

Jenny.

Not just Jenny, but Jenny kissing a pig, of all things. Nate laid the cookies on the hall table, then turned on a light so he could see the paper better. He blinked in the sudden brightness.

How long had it been since he'd had the lights on? That alone was a sign he'd spent too much time sleeping and not enough time —

No, he wasn't going to go there. He rested his weight against the wall and traced the grainy outline of her face.

Jenny.

How many years had it been? Almost ten. He would have thought she'd be married, living anywhere but Mercy by now.

But, no, the caption said "Third-grade teacher Jenny Wright." She was still single. Still his Jenny.

He shook his head. She hadn't been his

in such a long time. His brain, though, seemed to forget that fact.

He chuckled a little at the image of her down on her knees, puckered up with Reginald, the kissing pig. The sound of his own laughter startled him, like suddenly hearing a foreign language.

He knew what his mother was up to. Between the cookies and the picture of Jenny, she was hoping he'd come around. Go back to being the old Nate again.

The thing no one understood was that he couldn't go back to being that Nate. No matter how much he wanted to. He'd left that man behind two weeks ago when he'd opted for an honorable discharge from the marines instead of spending the rest of his service years behind a desk — the only other option the doctors gave him.

The doorbell rang and Nate jumped, dropping the paper to the floor. It fluttered apart, dispersing like feathers. He ignored the cane and hopped the few steps to the door on one foot. Through the glass panel, he could see who it was before he even opened the oak door.

He rubbed at his eyes. Surely, this was too coincidental to be true. Maybe he *had* been alone too long. Now he was starting to hallucinate. Next, it would be pink elephants.

The bell rang again.

Okay, the sound was real. The person on his porch had to be real, too, not a dream come to life.

Nate turned the knob and opened the door. "Hello, Jenny," he said, as if it had been ten minutes, not ten years, since he'd last seen her.

God, she looked beautiful. Even more so now with the sophistication of age. Her straight blond hair fell in a shimmering curtain against her neck and shoulders. She wore a suit of soft peach over a white silk blouse and matching pumps, as if she'd just come from church. Knowing Jenny, she probably had. Family and commitments had always been important to her, no matter the day of the week.

The nether parts of his body could care less how she was dressed. All he saw when he looked at her was a memory from ten years ago — Jenny lying on the back seat of his Grand Am, looking at him with a happy, satisfied smile and a love in her emerald eyes he'd thought would never die.

But that had been a long, long time ago. And he'd been wrong about the love part.

She tucked several strands of hair behind

her ear. He knew the gesture well. She was nervous. For some reason, that made him feel better. "Hi, Nate."

"Uh, you want to come in?"

She shook her head. "You're probably busy."

"Not especially. I could put on some coffee." If he *had* any coffee. He wasn't sure what was in his cabinets. He had cookies, though, and he could scrounge up something to drink to go with them.

"Okay, but only for a minute. I just wanted to stop by and discuss the game plan for next week."

He opened the door and waved her in. "Next week?"

She stopped in the hall. "Yeah, that's when you're scheduled to come into my classroom and help out, remember?"

He hadn't been in that deep of a fog, had he? "What are you talking about?"

"Dr. Davis told me you called the school and volunteered to help with my third-graders."

He shut the door and leaned against the wall so she wouldn't know how much his knee was hurting him. The last thing he wanted to do was drag out the cane in front of her. "Who's Dr. Davis?"

"The principal." Jenny put a hand to her

mouth. "You mean . . . you never talked to her?"

"No."

"Then how . . ." Her voice trailed off, confusion knitting her brows.

Nate glanced at the paper on the floor, the cookie tin on the hall table. It didn't take a master puzzler to put the pieces together. "My mother is behind this. I'm sure of it."

"Why would she do something like that?"

"She thinks I need something to keep me busy."

"You?" Jenny let out a laugh. "You're Type-A-plus. I can't imagine you ever sitting around doing nothing." Then she paused, as if her vision had finally adjusted to the darker interior. He saw her note the piles of dirty dishes in the kitchen behind him, the laundry he hadn't bothered to deal with beside the sofa, the discarded newspapers and empty pizza boxes tossed around the room.

"Ah, excuse the mess, I've been —" he cut himself off. What reason could he give? He'd been wallowing quite well in self-pity for the last couple of weeks? He'd lost all sense of direction and purpose? That he'd had a hell of a time knowing who he was since he'd returned to Mercy?

Better to leave the sentence unfinished.

Jenny started backing toward the door. "Well, I'm sorry for bothering you. I'll tell Dr. Davis it was all a big misunderstanding."

She was going to leave. If she did, he had a feeling it would be another ten years before he saw her again. And next time, her last name might not be Wright anymore.

"Jenny, wait." He took a step forward, then saw the cane against the wall, a stark reminder of why he was home in the first place.

She pivoted, her hand on the doorknob. "What?"

He tightened his fists at his side and gritted his teeth. "It was, ah, really nice to see you again."

A strange look flitted through her eyes. Disappointment? Hurt? He couldn't be sure. Half of him wanted to take the words back, to say something that would keep her here, but the other half disagreed.

"Yeah, you, too," she said. "Tell your mother I said hello."

And then she was gone. When the door shut, Nate turned off the hall light, yanked the cane up, and retreated to the sofa again. But for the first time, his sanctuary offered no comfort. Like a spring that wouldn't stay down, the memory of Jenny inside his hallway kept popping up and poking at him.

By the time he picked up the phone, he'd already half made up his mind.

Chapter Two

★ ★ ★

On Monday morning, Jenny came in early. She'd come up with seventeen ways of telling Dr. Davis that Nate had turned her down, but rejected them all. Even if the whole thing had been a scheme by Grace Dole to reunite the two of them, or a grand idea to get Nate out of the house, Jenny knew she had to find a way to make the whole thing work out, for the sake of her class. If she came up with a good enough excuse for his absence, then it could buy her enough time to convince Nate to change his mind.

David Copperfield moved mountains. Surely she could get one stubborn marine to agree to help her class — and her career. She'd already kissed a pig. How much worse could convincing Nate be?

But being around him . . . all day, every day. In the same room, within touching distance. Could she do that? Ten years ago, he'd been the man she'd wanted to marry.

The one she had laughed with, cried with. Kissed as if the world was going to end tomorrow.

Their world did. He'd joined the marines at seventeen and stopped coming home as often. The distance had made their bond weaker, not stronger. And eventually, one of them — she no longer remembered who — had said the words *break up,* and before she knew it, the dream she'd held for so many years had evaporated like summer rain on hot pavement.

It was better that way. She was happier. Granted, she was alone, but she no longer pounced on the mail truck, hoping for a letter or some sign that he was okay. That he still cared. She'd finally gone back to normal life.

Well, as normal as life could be with pink hair and a pig for a date.

Jenny pulled out a selection of new library books from her tote bag and set them up on a stand inside the reading circle.

"Miss Wright?"

Jenny wheeled around at the sound of Dr. Davis's voice. Already? She hadn't had time to prepare speech number eighteen yet. "Good morning, Dr. Davis."

"Is Mr. Dole here yet?"

"No, he, ah, he couldn't make it."

Dr. Davis arched an eyebrow. "Really? I was under the impression he was eager to help."

"I think your idea of bringing him in was a wonderful one," Jenny began, weaving speeches number two and number eleven together on the fly, "and I think the kids would really respond to something like that. The boys' top choices in books are almost always hero-related."

The other woman frowned. "I can hear a 'but' in your voice."

"But unfortunately, Mr. Dole —"

"Was running a little late this morning." Nate entered the room, bearing his weight against a cane. A cane? She hadn't noticed one yesterday.

Had he been injured? If so, that would explain why gung-ho, always-another-mission-to-take-on Nate was home for more than a minute.

She'd expected him to wear his uniform and was surprised to see him instead in a light-blue dress shirt and navy pants. He looked good, always had. Her heart, which didn't seem to listen to her head or the warning siren telling her not to notice how he looked, skipped a beat at the sight of him.

"My apologies, Miss Wright and Dr. Davis." He nodded toward each of them.

"I'm glad you could make it." The principal extended her hand to shake his. "Miss Wright was under the impression you weren't coming."

"Just a misunderstanding." He grinned. "I'm here and ready to help."

"Good. I'll get out of your way then." Dr. Davis gave him a smile, then left the room.

Once the principal was gone, Jenny turned to Nate. His face, she'd realized yesterday, looked older now, more tired, as if the weight of the world wasn't sitting so easily on his shoulders anymore. For a fleeting second, she wanted to reach out and make it easier for him.

She quickly shook off the thought. The days when she'd supported Nate were far in the past, and she intended to leave them that way. "What are you doing here?" she asked.

"Helping you."

"When I left yesterday, you didn't seem interested."

"I, ah, had some time to think it over." He took a seat on the edge of a desk. "I'm here for a week. Do with me what you will." He grinned.

A week. She could last a few days in his presence and not lose her mind or her heart again.

Couldn't she?

Jenny crossed her arms and leaned against the blackboard. "I don't buy it. You're as stubborn as a mule and once you've made up your mind, you never change it."

"It's been a long time, Jenny," he said quietly. "People change."

"Yes, they do." She picked up a piece of chalk and turned it over and over in her palm. "Sometimes."

The silence stood between them like a gate waiting to be unlocked. His deep-brown gaze met hers and she had to look away before all the thoughts she'd had over the last ten years came rushing to the sur-face.

I am over him.

But when she turned again to draw in the face that had once been as familiar as her own, she knew Nate wasn't the only liar in the room.

"Knock, knock." Debbie stuck her head in the room. "Oh, hi. I didn't know you had company, Jenny."

"Come on in." Jenny stepped forward and waved the other third-grade teacher into the room. If she had to, she would have dragged Debbie in. Anything to ease the growing tension between herself and Nate.

It's over between us. Maybe she needed to put that on a sign and wear it around her neck as a reminder.

"I'm Nate Dole," he said, putting out his hand to the slim brunette. "I'm here to help with Jenny's class for a few days."

Debbie's hazel eyes sparked to life and a wide smile took over her face when she took his hand in hers. "Well, if you ever run out of things to do, my classroom's right next door."

"I'll keep that in mind," Nate said. Their handshake — which seemed to last for hours — finally ended.

Jenny shouldn't have felt an ounce of jealousy. Nate had every right to flirt with another woman, kiss another woman, marry another —

No, his left hand was bare. He was still single.

She would *not* acknowledge the relief that flooded her at that thought.

"Well," Jenny said. "Mr. Dole and I need to re-organize the day. The children will be here in seventeen minutes and once they arrive, there won't be any time to breathe."

"Yeah, I better get to my own class." But Debbie didn't move.

Jenny opened the connecting door. "See you at lunch."

"Oh, yeah, lunch." Debbie shook her head, then turned to Nate. "Will you be here at lunch?"

"If Jenny wants me to be," he said.

Both of them turned to look at her. She wondered what was on the menu today and if Debbie would look good wearing it, then bit back the evil-twin thoughts. She was *not* jealous. Not one bit. "He doesn't have to stay *all* day."

"Oh, too bad," Debbie said. "I'm sure the . . . the, ah, students will really enjoy him being around. A big, tall guy like you." She gave him a smile and leaned against the doorframe. "You're a marine, I hear."

"Debbie?" Jenny said, laying the hint heavy in her voice. "I really need to rework my lesson plan for today."

"Yeah, sure. Me, too." Debbie dispensed another smile Nate's way, toothy as a Miss America contestant. "Have a nice day. If you need anything —"

"You're right next door," he finished for her.

Jenny distinctly heard the sound of Debbie sighing as she disappeared into her own classroom. With a firm shove, Jenny shut the door.

"Now, let's talk about the real reason why you're here," she began. "It's not altruism."

He grinned at her, as if he'd seen the spark in her eyes when Debbie had flirted with him. "To help you."

"I know you, Nate. You and children mix about as well as an elephant in a roomful of mice. I don't think so." She tapped her lip with her finger. "There's more to you showing up here than a nudge from your mother. I'd be willing to bet on it."

"Maybe." His grin widened, giving nothing away. "If you want to bet, we could make it interesting."

"This is an elementary school, remember? Nothing R-rated allowed."

"Too bad."

Jenny got out a stack of math fact review worksheets and began putting one on each child's desk for early-morning work. It was easier to do that than to focus on the teasing glint in his eyes. "Believe me, you won't be having any R-rated thoughts in a little while. Once those kids get hold of you, your brain will become mush and your body will beg for a nap."

"I've been through wars. I can handle a bunch of kids."

"A war is nothing compared to twenty-five third-graders."

"Jenny, I'm a marine, remember? I can handle it, believe me."

She paused and turned to him. "I'm going to take such pleasure in saying 'I told you so' later on today." She thrust the pile at him. "Here, finish putting these on the desks so I can get the vocabulary words up on the board."

He slid off the desk and hobbled to where his cane lay resting against the wall. When he'd entered the room, she'd seen him walking with it, but then she'd forgotten about it.

Her attention had been riveted on his face. Those liquid chocolate eyes. The way his hands moved when he talked. And that grin. That damned grin that even now, ten years later, could still cause an odd quiver in her heart.

"What happened to you?" She gestured to the cane.

He shook his head. "Just a little knee surgery. Nothing big."

Once again, she got the feeling he was holding something back, as if he had a bunch of secrets tucked in his back pocket. The Nate she'd known years ago had been as open as a pool of water. But the Nate she saw today had become a darker lake, filled with depths she couldn't see.

"Does it hurt?"

"Only when I let it."

Asking more would mean getting close to Nate. Treading in the personal zone. She didn't want to go there, not again. It had taken her two years to get over their breakup. She didn't have the heart to go down that path a second time.

"As an aide, all you really have to do is help any kids who are struggling." Jenny turned to the board and began writing because it was too hard to watch him wrangle his way through the rows of desks. She knew Nate — help was a four-letter word in his vocabulary. She cleared her throat and got to work chalking the list of words from the books the class had been reading. "Anyway, our theme this week is heroes. You being here is perfect timing."

"Why?"

She turned, the chalk still between her fingers. "Because you're the definition of a hero."

Nate shook his head. "Not in my Webster's." He jerked away, the cane rapping against the tile.

"Nate, what do you mean by —"

"Hi, Miss Wright," Jimmy Brooks said.

"My mom dropped me off early. Again."
The wiry blond boy disappeared behind
the coatroom wall, then poked his head
out. "Hey, who are you?" He pointed at
Nate.

"Jimmy, this is Master Sergeant Dole.
He's going to be with our class this week."

Jimmy dropped his backpack to the
floor. His eyes widened. "You're in the
army? Like a GI Joe?"

"I'm not —" Nate began.

"Mr. Dole is a marine," Jenny explained
before turning to Nate. "Sorry, I didn't
mean to interrupt you."

"That's, ah, exactly what I was going to
say anyway." Something flickered in his
eyes — a shadow passing through — but
then it was gone.

"How many people have you shot? Can I
see your gun?" Jimmy circled around Nate,
rat-a-tatting the questions.

"Later," Jenny said, bending down to the
boy's level to get his attention. "Right now,
you need to put your book bag away and
start your morning work. Sergeant Dole
will be here all week. You can talk to him
later."

"But —"

Jenny put up a finger. "I said later. And
no questions about shooting people."

"Aw, Miss Wright. You're no fun." Jimmy trudged off, muttering about how the class finally had someone cool and the teacher had made it all uncool.

She glanced at Nate and caught him watching her, a bemused expression on his face. Unbidden, the corners of her lips turned up into a smile. His brown gaze linked with hers, and something fluttered deep inside her. Something she'd thought she'd left in the past, like the photo album tucked under her bed.

Before Jenny could consider what that *something* could be, the bell rang and in gaggles like baby geese, the other children entered the room, talking and laughing, poking and prodding, complaining and shouting. Each stopped and stared when they noticed Nate, then started up a sea of whispers in the coatroom.

"As soon as you all take your seats and get your morning work done, I'll tell you about our visitor," Jenny called over the clamor. Focus on the class, not Nate. And maybe that quivering in her gut would stop.

The children nearly knocked each other over trying to get to their desks. Pencils flew across papers faster than cars zipping around the Indy 500 raceway. Like dominoes in reverse, one hand after the other shot up into the air, signaling they were done.

"If I'd known a visitor would get you all to work this hard, I would have brought one in a lot sooner," she said, laughing as she collected their papers. She waved Nate up to the front of the room. "Class, this is Master Sergeant Nathaniel Dole. He grew up in Mercy and even went to this school. He's a marine and he's visiting our class this week, as part of our reading project on heroes."

There were several exclamations of "Cool!" from the back of the room, a couple of yawns and several whispers between the children.

"Now, I'm sure you all have questions for Sergeant Dole. We'll do a brief question-and-answer period today and maybe another one tomorrow. Now, who has a question?"

A dozen hands reached upward, fingers wiggling. Jenny laughed and gave Nate's shoulder a pat. "You're on," she whispered.

Nate got to his feet and eyed the crowd. "What do I do?" he whispered to her.

"Just be honest. If there's one thing a kid can spot from fifty paces, it's an adult telling a lie. No gory stories, of course, but

41

you can tell them the truth. The goal here is to get them more interested in heroes so they'll want to read about them, too."

Nate shook his head. She had him confused with the man he used to be. "I'm not the right man for that."

"You're perfect." Jenny gave Nate a long, slow smile that ricocheted through him with the force of a hurricane wind. "The one thing you always did well was be a marine."

If she only knew, he thought, *how right she was.*

He wasn't a marine anymore, not the kind he'd dreamed of being. And thanks to the bullet that had torn through his knee, he never would be again.

Jenny walked over to her desk, leaving Nate to face the class alone. He pointed first to a little girl with blond hair who seemed to have a continual sniffle. "What's your question?"

She dabbed at her nose with a crumpled tissue. "What's a marine do?"

He drew himself up and gave her a nod. "Good question. The grunts are the first ones into the hot spots. For instance, we'd take a beachhead with an amphibious assault and cordon off an LZ, then . . ." His voice trailed off as he noticed the furrowed brows surrounding him. "Uh, we go in first when there's a war and make a safe place for planes to land the other troops." He pointed next to a small boy with glasses.

"What happened to your leg? How come you got to have a cane?"

"I, ah, had some knee surgery." Not exactly a lie. Not quite the truth, either, but there were some things he wasn't ready to talk about, Jenny's advice about being honest be damned.

"Where's your gun?" Jimmy interrupted, before he could be called on.

"I don't carry it when I'm not on duty." He pointed to a girl in the back row who had her hair in twin pigtails. His mother, he remembered, had always done his sister's hair like that.

For a second, he felt a pang at not having seen Katie since he came home. He missed her and his brothers — Jack, Luke, Mark. All were married now, settled down with families — nieces and nephews he barely knew because he'd been gone from Mercy more often than not.

He shook his head and, with skills honed over years of being apart from his family, Nate brushed the thought away. His mother had been calling and asking him over, but he'd made one excuse after another. He'd see his sister and brothers when he was ready. When he could somehow explain the man he'd become.

He was far from being able to do that right now.

"I'm sorry, I didn't hear your question," he said to the little girl.

"If you're a marine, how come you're not dressed like one?" she asked. "How come you're not wearing your uniform?"

Nate's grip on the cane tightened. The muscles in his jaw formed into immovable lumps, as if someone had injected them with concrete.

The question wasn't a hard one. But it required an answer more complicated than he could give to a group of nine-year-olds at eight-thirty in the morning.

"I just decided to wear something else today," he said finally.

"Can you wear your uniform to-morrow?" Jimmy asked. "I bet it's really cool. Do you have a lot of medals and stuff?"

He'd *had* medals. Past tense. He thought of the dark-blue coat, once hung with ribbons and golden pins whispering of past deeds.

But now . . .

Now he didn't wear it anymore. It had

been far too painful a reminder, so he'd stuffed it into the dark recesses of his closet. A few months ago, that uniform had been his life. He didn't have the athletic prowess of Mark, the brains of Luke, the business acumen of Katie or the focus of Jack. Nate thrived on action, adventure. And the only thing he seemed to be good at, since the Christmas he got his first GI Joe, was battling the bad guys — and winning.

Now that he wasn't wearing the clothes of a marine, he felt lost, as if he wasn't sure what uniform he was supposed to wear anymore.

"Can you wear your marine clothes tomorrow? I bet it's really awesome," another boy said.

"No." Nate's voice came out tight and strangled. He cleared his throat and tried again. "No, I can't wear it."

"Why not?"

"Yeah, why not?"

He cast a help-me look at Jenny. She grinned at him and stepped forward. "That's enough questions for today," she said. "It's eight-forty-two. Time to get started on our vocabulary words. Now, everybody copy down . . ."

While she talked, Nate scooted around

the desks and made his way to the back of the room. He slipped his free hand into his pocket and fingered the piece of paper that had arrived that morning on his fax machine. Whether he liked it or not, he had to stay in Jenny's class for the entire week.

After Jenny had left, he'd called his V.A. doctor, thinking the physician would tell Nate he had a good reason to go on staying at home and off his knee. But no, the doctor had disagreed, and when the story of Jenny's visit had slipped out, he'd ordered Nate to a week in Jenny's class as "therapy" for his knee. Whether this was going to be good for him or not remained to be seen.

Looking at the wide-eyed, eager faces around him, he realized Jenny had been right.

These kids were going to eat him alive.

Chapter Three

★ ★ ★

"I think I should alert the Pentagon," Nate said to Jenny after morning recess a couple of hours later.

She laughed, the sound of it as light and airy as clouds skipping across the sky. He had always loved the sound of her laughter. There had been a lot of things he'd realized he'd missed when he came back home, but none caused the wrench of longing in his gut the way Jenny's laughter did. "Why do you say that?"

"You've got this classroom running better than a lot of platoons. I've never seen such organization, especially with kids."

She pulled open the door to her classroom and waved the children inside. Nate stayed on the opposite side of the stoop, providing crowd control. "You should see me the first day. It's all chaos until I get to know the kids and they get to know me."

"I bet you have a schedule and a routine all set before the first bell rings on opening day. If I remember right, you weren't the type to like chaos for very long."

The last child skipped across the threshold, followed by Nate. Jenny swung the door shut and latched it firmly. "No, I didn't." Her voice had dropped into a softer, almost melancholy range.

Jenny's childhood, he knew, had been a topsy-turvy one. She'd never talked about it much, but it had been clear her flighty mother and absent father had made her young life unpredictable. Throughout their courtship, she'd called Nate her "rock," the one support system she could count on. With him, Jenny had seemed to let loose, live more for the moment, as if she trusted him to be there when she needed to come back to reality.

Inevitably, though, she'd always rein herself back in, focusing on work or homework or whatever else was more important then, as if she'd suddenly realized the consequences of being too spontaneous. They'd had fun when they'd dated, most of the time, when Jenny had let down her hair and really let him into her heart and her world.

He remembered the fights, the days when it seemed there was no way to repair the damage between himself and Jenny, but he also remembered so much more. Laughter over nothing at all. Hugs on the porch. Kisses sneaked behind the shed. Teasing, torturous touches in the lake during summer camp.

"Jenny, I —"

She turned to him, her emerald eyes wide. Waiting. "Yes?"

Save for a slight maturity in her face and a lightening in her hair, Jenny Wright was the same woman he remembered. Her laughter, her smile, her eyes. All of it exactly the same, as if the past ten years had passed in a blink.

But *he* was different. And he'd be fooling himself if he thought she'd want anything but the old Nate, the strong, can-do-anything man he'd been. That was the man she had loved, not the shell of a used-up soldier he'd become. "Never mind."

"Don't do that. You were about to say something. Tell me."

He looked past her, into the bright and sunny classroom that so captured Jenny's personality in the vibrant wall hangings and the sunflowers decorating the bulletin boards. "I . . . I think Jimmy is trying to feed Lindsay a worm."

"Oh, God, not again," she muttered and spun away.

Within thirty seconds, she had the offensive invertebrate back outside, Lindsay calmed and Jimmy seated at a desk in the hall. "Exile worked well with Napoleon," Jenny explained, joining Nate at the back of the room. "And it works well with Jimmy Brooks, too."

"You're a genius."

"Nah, I just have a system that works for me. All teachers do." She glanced at her watch, then stepped away from him, clapped her hands and two dozen heads popped to attention. "Story time, children. Everyone grab a mat and take a seat on the floor. Today, we'll read together instead of having a silent reading period."

A few minutes of scrambling, and then the class had assembled in a circle on the floor around a small rocking chair. Jenny grabbed a book off the shelf and pressed it into Nate's hands. "Here you go."

"What do you want me to do with this?"

"Wear it." She grinned. "No. Read to them."

"Me?"

"That's what you're here for." She leaned closer and the scent of sandalwood wafted up to greet him. In the bottom of his foot locker was a box of letters that held that very scent, faint now after all these years, but still discernible if he placed them very, very close to his face.

How many times had he done that in those lonely years in the marines? Those days after he'd lost her, when the only thing he'd had was a few sheets of sandalwood-scented stationery? Too many times, he knew.

He jerked himself back to the present when he saw her staring at him. "What'd you say?"

"I said, go read to them before they start a riot in the circle." She gestured to the group of kids, already starting to argue and tease each other.

He grinned. "Your wish is my command."

Jenny smiled back. "Now why can't all men say that more often?"

"Because we rarely mean it." He caught her chuckle as he made his way through the crowd of children, who parted like the Red Sea to make room for him and his cane to wriggle through. Once he was settled in the chair, he cracked open the story and began to read.

At first, his voice droned in a monotone, the cadenced speech pattern he'd developed after so many years in the military. But then, as the pages passed and the story began to grow more interesting, Nate slipped into the voices of the characters, adding inflections to the old man, high pitches to the shrieking neighbor woman and a deep baritone for the firefighter who all starred in the tale.

The children stopped squirming and talking. They perched their elbows on their knees and leaned forward, ears pitched toward the sound of his voice. When he reached the last page, several of them let out cries of disappointment.

"Let's thank Mr. Dole for his spirited reading debut," Jenny said, stepping into the circle.

The applause that encircled him could have been coming from Carnegie Hall. Nate shut the book. "It was fun."

"I told you so," she whispered, taking the novel from him and replacing it on the shelf. "You always were a ham."

The children got to their feet, replacing their carpeted mats in the pile and heading back to their seats. Jenny grabbed a stack of worksheets off her desk and handed them out, directing the class to write a short paragraph on the story and draw a picture of their favorite character.

Nate came up beside her. "I was not a ham," he said.

Jenny laid the extra sheets on her desk and quirked a brow at him. "Who starred in every production put on by the Mercy Elementary Players?"

He chuckled. "I don't think playing the lead in *You're a Good Man, Charlie Brown* qualifies me for Oscar status."

"You loved it. Admit it. I'm surprised you didn't go into acting."

He let out a snort. "There's plenty of that in the marines, believe me. Pretend the drill instructor doesn't make you so mad you want to scream until your voice gives out. Pretend the food in the mess hall doesn't taste like something left over from the Dark Ages. Pretend you don't miss the people back home so much you can barely sleep at night."

She toyed with the pencils in a white Hug a Teacher mug on her desk. "Did you?"

"Did I what?"

"Miss . . . people?"

"Yeah," he said quietly. "A lot of them."

"Miss Wright?" A little boy in the second-to-last row raised his hand.

She got to her feet and left her desk, as if she were grateful for the change of subject. "Yes, Lionel?"

"How do you spell *grenade launcher?*"

"Why? There weren't any weapons in the story."

"I know. I'm writing about Sergeant Dole instead. He's cool. I even got a picture of him killing the —"

"Lionel, that wasn't your assignment."

"Yeah, but, I'm writing a story." He raised his paper as proof. All of the lines were filled in with neat, tight script. "And didn't you always say it's not so important what we read and write about, but that we're reading and writing?"

"Well, yes, but —"

"This is what I want to write about." He turned and replaced his paper on his desk, pencil at the ready. "So can you tell me how to spell *grenade launcher?*"

"Some interesting reading material for today?"

Nate saw Jenny pivot toward the woman who'd entered the room. "Dr. Davis!" she said. "I didn't hear you come in."

"Apparently not." She looked down her glasses, surveyed the classroom, then crooked a finger in Jenny's direction. Jenny crossed the room and met the principal at the door. "What were you reading to these children today?" Dr. Davis asked.

"This is heroes' week. Our first book was about a firefighter who rescued a family."

Jenny withdrew the novel from the shelf and handed it to the principal. The two of them moved into the hall, leaving the door ajar.

Dr. Davis flipped through the pages and harrumphed. "Then why are the children writing stories about war weapons?"

"They're not —"

"Jenny is an excellent teacher," Nate interjected in a soft tone, joining them. "She gets these students motivated and hasn't taught them anything inappropriate. The grenade-launcher thing came about because the kids heard I was in the marines and one boy decided to write a story about me instead of the assignment."

"I was about to explain the right way to do their worksheet," Jenny said.

"I hope you don't think it would be fun," on this word, Dr. Davis directed a pointed glance at Jenny, "to share war escapades with these impressionable minds."

"No, ma'am, I did not," Nate replied. "Miss Wright, in fact, kept everything away from that focus."

"Well," Dr. Davis said after a moment. "That's a relief." She handed the book back to Jenny, then left.

Jenny poked her head back into the room. "Class, continue working on your

assignment, doing it the way I told you to."
She gave Lionel a pointed glance. "I need
to talk to Master Sergeant Dole in the
hall."

A few voices uttered the fatal "Uh-oh"
as Jenny shut the door a little more to
block prying eyes and ears.

She crossed her arms over her chest. "I
don't need you to fight my battles for me."

"Against Dr. Dragon Lady?" he said. "I
think you could use all the allies you can
get."

Another teacher came striding down the
hall. Jenny lowered her voice. "Nate, don't
come marching in here and try to fix my
life like it's old times. I don't need you to
take charge anymore. I'm a big girl now."

"I wasn't trying to do that."

"Oh, yeah?"

He took a step closer to her, invading her
space, putting a chink in the wall of invul-
nerability she had built up in the years
since they'd broken up. "Yeah."

With that one word, the air between
them hushed. For a moment, she was lost
in the depths of his eyes, her heart racing
like a hummingbird. He grinned at her, the
same easy grin that had always made her
melt. The smile reached his eyes, softening
the hard lines put there by his years in the

military. For a moment, he became the Nate she remembered. The Nate she couldn't say no to.

The Nate she'd —

Jenny heard the click-click of heels against linoleum and looked away. Dr. Davis was coming back around the corner, heading down the hallway toward her classroom.

Oh, no.

She considered grabbing Nate and ducking back into the room before the principal reached them — until she glimpsed a familiar pair of overalls coming toward her from the opposite direction.

Oh, God. The Animals Where You Want 'Em guy. He'd probably come to collect on his payment after all.

But no, he had something with him. Something smaller than a pig. And furrier, too. In fact, it looked a lot like —

A goat.

"Is that what I think it is?" Nate asked, his whisper warm against her ear.

"I really, really hope not," Jenny said.

Dr. Davis's heels clicked toward them from one end of the hall, the goat's four hooves clacked from the opposite direction. It was like watching an approaching tidal wave and being powerless to stop it before it took out the defenseless coastal bungalow.

"Hide me," Jenny said to Nate, ducking behind his broad back.

"Hide you? From what?"

"From the goat that's about to eat my career."

Chapter Four

★ ★ ★

"Sir! You can't bring that, that *thing* in here," Dr. Davis called. "Get it out of my school immediately."

"No, ma'am, no can do. It's too late." Ed Spangler stopped, gesturing behind him, grinning like a gold medalist in the Olympics. "We're already going to be famous."

If ever there was a time for the floor to open up and devour her, this was it. The photographer from the *Mercy Daily News* stood behind Ed, camera at the ready.

"What?" Dr. Davis sputtered. "You can't . . . you won't . . . *you wouldn't.*"

Ed turned to Jenny, who'd realized she couldn't hide any more from her fate. "Miss Wright, when you kissed my Reginald, it turned my business upside down and inside out. I haven't gotten so many calls since my cow Eloise ran down the center of Main Street with Larry Bertram's bull in hot pursuit, if you get my drift."

Dr. Davis blanched. Beside her, Jenny saw Nate suppressing a chuckle.

"This here is Miss BoJangles, my Tennessee Fainting Goat. She's harmless and cute as a button, but she has a bit of stage fright. If you could kiss her, too, for the papers, it might just turn her career around." He gave Nate a jab with his elbow. "Not to mention put Animals Where You Want 'Em on the map."

"I can't go around kissing every animal on your farm," Jenny said.

"Sure you can. Besides, this one's a real cutie." Ed gave the tan-and-white goat a little push so she was only a few inches from Jenny.

The children had crowded around the door of the classroom, poking their heads out and watching the commotion. "Kiss her, Miss Wright!"

That was the last thing she needed — commentary from the third-grade peanut gallery.

"Remove this goat," Dr. Davis said. "It's disrupting my school."

"I'd read five books to see Dr. Davis kiss a goat," Jimmy Brooks said to Lionel, his voice low but not so low that the adults didn't overhear him, too.

Alex snorted. "I'd read seven. Ten if we

could get that cow in here."

Jenny shot a glare at the boys. She'd be lucky if she'd be able to find a job giving Yahtzee lessons at the community center when this was over.

Dr. Davis backed up a step. "Get that animal out of my school. Now!"

"Hey, keep it down." The man waved a shushing hand at them. "She faints when she gets scared."

Jenny's career was self-destructing right there in the hallway. On one side were the students, cheering her on to kiss the goat. On another, the photographer, ready to capture the moment and blast it all over the front page. Completing the unemployment-line triangle was Dr. Davis, her face turning more crimson with every passing second.

And then there was Nate, who'd come up beside her, silently offering his support. He was a breath away from her shoulder, his presence both a comfort and a distraction. For a second, it felt like old times — her and Nate against the world.

"If it was me, and I was up against this enemy," he whispered with a tease in her ear, "I'd turn the situation to my advantage."

She turned to look at him. "How?"

"Use the power of the press," Nate said. Their gazes connected. A light bulb went off in her brain. She gave him a smile of gratitude, which he returned with one that sent a shiver of hot adrenaline through her.

Focus on the problem, not on Nate, even if Nate was part of the problem — at least the problem causing all the turmoil in her gut.

"I'll kiss the goat," Jenny announced. "But only if you also run a story on Dr. Davis and her *great* support of the teachers at this school." She stepped to the right, looped her arm into the principal's, and smiled big.

The photographer raised his lens and snapped the picture before Dr. Davis could protest. "Can you say that again, so I can get a quote for the caption?" He withdrew a pad and pen from his chest pocket.

"Certainly." Jenny repeated her statement and spelled their names. "Dr. Davis has implemented a wonderful program to help boost our school's reading scores," she added.

The principal's eyebrows arched in surprise. For the first time since Jenny had met her, Dr. Davis seemed to be at a loss for words.

Jenny had won that skirmish. Nate gave

her a grin of triumph and it felt as if the hall had done a 360-degree turn around her. "You forgot something," he whispered.

"What?"

"You owe someone a kiss."

For a second, she thought he meant him. The anticipation of pressing her mouth against his for the first time in almost a decade roared through her veins.

Despite it all, she *had* missed him. His eyes. His smile. His —

"Miss BoJangles is waiting for her shot at stardom," Nate said.

The goat. He'd meant the silly goat. "Oh. Oh, yeah." Jenny swallowed and bent down to the omnivore, pretending she wasn't disappointed at all. "You ready, Miss BoJangles?"

The goat let out a "baa" and skittered back a couple of steps.

"She's nervous," Ed explained. "It's her first kiss."

"Mine, too. With a goat anyway." Her first kiss at all in a long, long while. Besides the pig, she amended. Maybe that's why she'd been reacting to Nate's presence like a bee around a new flower. Yeah, that was all it was.

Jenny bent down, leaned forward. The

photographer trained his lens on them.

"Kiss the goat! Kiss the goat!" the kids chanted again.

The goat's eyes widened.

"Yeah, kiss her," Nate whispered in her ear, and when he did, Jenny knew she was kidding herself if she thought the next few days were going to be a breeze. With Nate around, she was in trouble. Big trouble. She'd be better off spending the week on Ed's farm with Reginald.

At that instant, the lunchtime bell rang. All the classroom doors were flung open at once, spilling lines of children into the hall in a flood of noisy shouts and chatter, exploding in volume when they noticed the farm animal in their midst.

The goat started, then collapsed on the floor, rolling to her back, her four legs jutting straight up like fuzzy toothpicks.

"Oh, damn. She's gone and fainted." Ed let out a gust. "*Now* how am I going to get my picture?"

When the final bell rang at the end of the day, grade 3-B dispersed like birds heading south for winter. They were gone in seconds, sweeping out of the room in a flurry of backpacks and shouted goodbyes. Nate took a seat on the edge of a desk and let out a sigh. "Is it like that every day?"

Jenny laughed. "Pretty much. You should be proud of yourself, though."

"Why's that?"

"You survived your first day of third grade." She grinned. The sunlight streaming in the broad windows on the far side of the room glinted off her golden hair like a halo. She reached up and twisted it into a ponytail, securing the hairdo with a rubber band she snagged off her desk. In half a second, Jenny seemed to transform from organized professional into —

The girl he used to know. And love. A long time ago.

Whoa. That was treading on territory best left untraveled.

"Yeah, I survived," Nate said. He'd also survived his first day being back with Jenny. He didn't know which had been harder — the exhausting children or the continual push-pull in his chest.

"It does get easier," she said.

"Does it?" Nate slipped off the desk and crossed to her.

"Yep. I promise. When I was a student teacher, I went home many days and said I was going to quit the next morning. Then some kid would be there waiting for me when I got into work and he'd smile at me, or she'd bring me a picture she drew at home. And I'd stay." Jenny's smile turned wistful and she took a long look around her room. "Seven years later, and I'm still here."

"You love what you do. That makes it easier."

"It does." She straightened, drawing her attention back to him. "I bet you miss the marines. I know you loved the military."

More important were the words left unsaid. He didn't speak them, didn't negate them. That was the past, and that was where it was going to stay.

"I miss it," was all he said.

"Well," she said, moving to her desk and stuffing a pile of papers into a tote bag. "You're not much of a conversationalist today."

"Sorry." He grinned. "I am a guy, you know. My ancestors were lucky to progress beyond grunts and raised fists."

She laughed. "I'm not so sure the four-word sentences are a big improvement." Jenny swung the tote over her shoulder and grabbed her spring jacket off the back of her chair.

"Where are you going?"

"Home. That's generally what I do at the end of the day."

"Don't."

"Don't go home? I did just spend more than eight hours here. Remember, they don't pay overtime to teachers." She chuckled. "I've got papers to grade, a quiz on Lewis and Clark to write up, a health *and* a science lesson to develop —"

"Forget it." He put up a hand to head off her protests. "Not forever. Just for today. Come with me. Go to dinner. Walk in the park."

She blinked. "Are you serious?"

Was he? Hadn't he five seconds ago vowed to stay uninvolved?

He looked again at the bag in her hands, the coat on her arm, and in that second knew that if she walked out the door and left him, it would be too easy to slip back into the man who'd spent his days warming the sofa cushions.

"Yeah, I'm serious."

"I have a lot to do. The class . . ." She shook her head and bit her lip. "No. I'm not going to finish that sentence. You're right. I never take time off. I never go out to dinner. You've made me an offer I can't — and won't — refuse. So, I'll go with you, on one condition."

"What's that?"

"You help me come up with a killer idea for health for tomorrow and a science project that will wow the kids on Friday and I'll be yours the rest of the day."

"Now that's an offer *I* can't refuse," Nate said, following her out of the classroom. "I take it anything that blows up, stinks or attracts wild animals is out?"

She chuckled as she shut off the lights and locked the door. "Yeah, I'd say so."

"Pity." They began walking together toward the exit of the building, their steps falling into a matched pattern, as if they did this every day. The image of them chatting and leaving the same place — then returning together in the morning — flitted through his mind.

Nope. Not going to go there. This was a temporary assignment. Nothing more. "Remember Miss Marchand's biology class?" he said, if only to bring up the least sexy thing he could think of.

"I remember studying my brains out every night, trying to pass."

"And studying with me because I was better at it than you."

She cast him a sideways glance, an eyebrow arched. "You weren't all that focused on biology when we studied together, if I remember right."

"That's because I had the hottest girl in

Mercy High as my study partner."

"I can't blame you for a lack of concentration, then." She gave him a smile he could have considered flirtatious.

"And studying you could be considered biology."

She laughed. "Not the flora and fauna kind."

"Oh, I thought about flora."

"You thought about taking me up to Makeout Hill with a blanket and a Bruce Springsteen tape."

"Hey, that was communing with nature." He grinned. "And you."

"Not exactly the kind of nature Miss Marchand had in mind for our homework assignments."

"You're right about that."

In a few steps and a handful of sentences, they'd fallen into the repartee they'd shared before, as natural as putting on a pair of shoes he'd had in the back of his closet. It felt good. But also scary. As if the shoes weren't quite the right ones anymore, and yet he still didn't want to give them up.

They weren't a couple anymore. And he didn't have any business trying to take them along that road.

"You know, Miss Marchand still goes

around town bragging about 'those Dole boys,' and how you, Jack, Mark and Luke were the only ones ever to ace her class." Jenny hit the bright sunshine of the parking lot and turned her face upward to greet the light. As long as he'd known her, Jenny had been a woman who always took a moment to greet the outdoors when she reached it. He, on the other hand, had always been too busy, in too much of a hurry to do more than hop on the next helicopter, flying off on the next mission.

Besides, enjoying sunshine and smelling the roses wasn't exactly cool in the marines.

Nate laughed. "I doubt that. Poor Katie. She tried hard, but biology wasn't her forte."

"You'd never know it to look at your sister today." Jenny gave him a grin as they crossed the still-full lot. Apparently the teachers at Mercy Elementary were used to putting in a few hours after the children went home. Across the fields behind them, older children were at soccer practice, running up and down between the goals after the elusive black-and-white ball. "Her twins are three now and I think she and Matt are thinking about having another, if they haven't already started."

He thought back to what the last letter from home had said about Katie. "My mother said Katie vowed after the twins she'd never have another kid again."

"Apparently Matt can be pretty persuasive." Jenny smiled. "And those twins, once they got past the terrible twos, are the cutest things on Earth. Who wouldn't want to have more like that?"

"Not me." He put up his hands. "I'm not kid material, especially after today."

"I disagree. You did great today. The kids really enjoyed having you there. You'd be even better with your own, I'm sure."

"I handle M-16s for a living, Jenny. Not baby wipes and diaper-rash creams."

"Same difference. Just different battles." She turned toward him again and grinned.

When she smiled at him like that, he thought anything was possible. Even that.

He cleared his throat and worked on making his way over the rough asphalt with his cane. He ignored the throbbing in his knee that told him he'd be better off sitting down instead of moving. "That's what my brothers say. Mark and Claire have a baby now; and I hear Luke and Anita are having fun raising their new son even though Emily's officially a teenager."

"You hear?"

Damn. Jenny didn't miss a thing. How had he let that slip by? "I ah, haven't talked to Luke recently." Or Mark or Jack or Katie or even his parents. But he didn't add those details.

"But haven't you been in town for a while?"

"I've been busy. Stuff for my knee." He waved the cane for evidence.

She gave him a dubious look but didn't ask any more. "I'm enjoying the walk. The weather's nice. I don't get outside for more than a couple of recesses a day and I really miss the outdoors."

"You sound like a hermit."

She laughed. "Far from it. Just your typical busy teacher. Too much to do. Not enough hours. If I'm playing hooky, I might as well do it right." She unlocked the door of an older red Chevy Malibu and dropped her tote bag onto the passenger's seat, then shut the door and locked it again. "There, I'm officially free. For a few hours at least."

"What about Lewis and Clark?"

She waved a hand. "Ah, they're dead. They don't mind waiting for me."

He laughed. He couldn't remember the last time he had laughed this much in one day. It had to have been years ago. Certainly not in the past few months. Not in the weeks since his knee had been blown apart by enemy fire and he'd been left half the man he used to be.

"Oh, wait," Jenny said. "I forgot. Your knee. Have you changed your mind about walking? Would you rather drive?"

The pain he'd felt a minute ago didn't seem so bad anymore. Not with her beside him, her face filled with concern. "Actually, my doctor would give you a standing ovation for helping me work it. I haven't been the most cooperative rehab patient."

"You? I find that hard to believe." She chuckled.

"You know me. I don't take direction well."

"You redefine being in charge, Nate."

He echoed her laughter. "Nothing like a day in a third-grade classroom to remind me how little I control."

They turned out of the school drive and took a right onto Clark Street. "Aw, you get used to it. Run a tight ship and things stay pretty much in control."

"Save for the occasional worm in someone's hair." The sun was warm, the weather in the high sixties, a bit unseasonably warm for Indiana in late March. But

Nate wasn't about to complain.

"Yeah, except for that. I try to avoid that kind of chaos."

"With more than two dozen nine-year-olds? Pretty impossible, if you ask me."

She shrugged. "Not if you have a good plan."

They passed a line of houses, neat and trim bungalow styles put here when Mercy was first formed. A few neighbors raised a hand in greeting as they walked by. "Always the same Jenny, aren't you? Organized, efficient. Chaos-free?"

"And what's wrong with that?"

"Nothing." They'd reached the corner of Cherry Street. Nate raised his arm to point out Katie's apartment, then realized Katie hadn't lived there in almost four years. She was married now. Living in the house Matt had built on the old Emery farm property.

To Nate, time seemed to stop whenever he left Mercy for Panama, Columbia, Kuwait — wherever the government needed him. With a pang, he realized things had moved on and changed, all when he hadn't been looking.

Jenny had changed, too. She'd had a life. Without him. One that no longer even needed him to take care of her, as she'd made quite clear to him today. Maybe he was crazy for thinking that she could be his again.

They strolled along the next block, then turned left onto Main Street. "Not a lot of choices here for dinner, same as always," Jenny said. "Maybe we should have driven. We could have gone to that bed and breakfast that's out on the outskirts of town, or headed into Lawford. For a real selection."

He grinned. "I forgot how small Mercy was."

"Hey, nine thousand people and growing. It's not that small."

"It's bigger than many of the places I've been stationed in. And the food's always been good, midwestern cooking." He paused, leaning slightly against a telephone pole so Jenny wouldn't know his knee had started up again. "My kind of place."

"It never was before."

He cleared his throat and looked away, down the short strip of downtown Mercy. "I meant for now."

"A pit stop for a little refueling before you go back to whatever war it is you're fighting these days, huh?"

He heard the familiar fight in her words. He could tell her he was out of the marines for good and take that fight away. But that would mean opening up a can of worms that he had no intention of dealing with. Not now. "Yeah."

She paused a moment, as if assessing whether she should ask him anything more. Then she shook her head, readjusted her purse on her shoulder and gestured toward Marge's Diner. "There's our best choice for dinner, other than the Corner Pocket bar and the Pizza Palace."

"They still only deliver on Tuesdays?"

"They added Saturdays, now that the owner hired a helper with a license." Jenny grinned. "Gotta love small town life. No conveniences."

"And no hassles from big cities."

"There is that." She smiled. Clearly, Jenny still loved the town of Mercy as much as she ever had. He wondered what it was like to love something that much. To be that attached to a place.

"If you're hungry now," she added, "we could eat first, then head over to the park with dessert."

"Marge's is fine. And I'm always ready to eat." Already though, he was regretting the decision. There was one thing a small town was good at — making someone get involved. The intimacy, the familiarity. It all came back and wrapped around him like vines drawing him closer to the one jungle he'd avoided.

"I love this restaurant, even though it's just a simple little diner," she said as they approached the small diner, its bright-blue awning hanging over the sidewalk in welcome. "My parents, grandparents and I used to eat here all the time when I was a kid. It was a lot easier than cooking at home, my mom always said."

How many times had Nate taken Jenny here when they'd been dating? How many meals and sundaes had they shared in the four years they'd been together? She hadn't mentioned any of that.

She'd forgotten. Or wanted to forget.

Nate held the door for her as she entered. "How are your parents and grandparents doing?"

"My mom moved to Arizona last year after her new husband retired. I think it might be their last move, but you know how she is. My mother can't stand to stay in the same place for more than five seconds. It's a wonder I lived in Mercy as long as I did when I was a kid."

"Didn't your folks buy three or four different houses, just in the time I was dating you?"

"Five. My mother was never known for

being a stable person." Jenny shook her head, as if she didn't want to revisit those years. "As for my grandparents, my grandfather moved to an apartment in Mercy a couple of years ago, but he's a lot more reclusive since my grandmother passed away and he sold their Lawford house. My dad was his only son and when he died eight years ago, then my grandmother passed away six years later, my grandfather sort of went into a shell. Now, he kind of sticks to himself. Doesn't want to get out like he used to. He's got a dog though, and the Lawford vet said he should get out and walk him."

"Because the dog's putting on some pounds?"

"No, because Spike's been feeling a little down. Or at least, that's what the vet told him." Jenny smiled. "I think Dr. McAllister saw Grandpa was feeling down, more than the dog. Gave him a canine prescription that was actually better for the master than the pet."

"And has he done it?"

A waitress came up and greeted them almost immediately. She recognized Jenny by name and gave Nate a hello. She raised an eyebrow at Jenny's male companion before seating them at a booth along the side wall that faced the street. The waitress — her name tag said she was Jodie — left them with menus, returning a second later with full glasses of ice water.

"Not yet," Jenny said. "But I'm going to go over there later this week and get him out and about one way or the other."

"Always determined, aren't you?"

"I learned that from the best, didn't I? You were the most determined man I ever knew." She slipped the slice of lemon off the side of her water glass, squeezed a couple of drops into the beverage, then dropped the lemon into her drink and stirred it with her straw. "Always knew what you wanted and went after it."

Everything but her, in the end. How could he explain how important the marines had been — hell, still was? How it made him feel, how it filled some hole in him that nothing else did?

"Nate Dole! Is that you?" Dave Brooks hurried over to their table. Without waiting for an invitation, he swung an empty chair from a nearby table over to their booth and plunked himself down. "How are you, buddy? I haven't seen you in what, ten, eleven years?"

Nate nodded and gave his old high-school friend a smile and clap on the shoulder. Still the same irrepressible grin on Dave's face, albeit under a chubbier face and thinner hairline. "It's been a while."

"So, you two back together? Or just catching up?" He arched his brows and gestured between them. "You two were always such an item. Surprised you didn't marry her while you had the chance. Now she's the most eligible bachelorette in Mercy."

"Under the age of seventy," Jenny added.

"Not to mention the prettiest." Dave gave her a grin.

Something Nate refused to name burned inside his gut. Dave was grinning at Jenny with familiarity, bred, Nate knew, of living in the same town all their lives. Years ago, the three of them had been friends. But now — was there something more?

"Nate and I are just working together this week," she said. "He's helping out in my classroom."

"You are? Hey, that means you've got my boy, Jimmy," he said to Nate.

"You've got a son?" Nate drew back in surprise. "You, of all people?"

"Yep. And a four-year-old daughter. Probably the last guy you expected to see as a dad. I figure my days as a party animal make me a stricter dad, though. I know how to outsmart the kids." He winked.

"Are you married, too?"

"I was. Five years to Kimberly Jenkins. But . . . things didn't work out. We got divorced four and a half years ago."

"Sorry to hear that."

"Yeah, what are you going to do? Now that I'm single again, pickings are slim around Mercy." He grinned again at Jenny. "I've been asking this one out for years, but she always turns me down."

"You know Lily over at the Corner Pocket has something for you, Dave." Jenny sent a thumb in the direction of the bar and pool hall, diagonally across the street from Marge's.

The other man's face turned a slight shade of red. "She's a good woman. Expects a lot out of me."

"As she should," Nate quipped. "You always needed to be kept in line."

"Hey, not as much as you, military boy. You always were the wild one."

"Not anymore. Those days are over."

Dave gave him a light jab. "Got old on me, did you?"

"Hey, I'm only twenty-nine. Not exactly ancient."

"Bumping up against thirty. That hill's

getting closer." Dave grinned.

"Before you both start making me feel like I should go sign up for Social Security," Jenny said, "why don't we change the subject? I'm the same age as the two of you."

"Aw, you don't look a day over twenty-one," Dave replied. "Still the prettiest girl in Mercy."

Dave had said that twice now. Nate had to restrain himself to keep from beating his former best friend into a pulp on the blue-and-white gingham tablecloth.

"So, how's my boy doing?" Dave asked. "He giving you any trouble?"

"He's all right," Jenny said. "Nothing to worry about."

"If you don't count the worm he tried to feed to Lindsay today," Nate added.

"Again?" Dave let out a gust. "I swear, that boy is going to turn me gray. It's just been so hard on him since the divorce. With Kim having primary custody, I don't get to see him as much as I would like."

Jenny laid a comforting hand on Dave's. Nate tried his damnedest not to care. "He's probably just acting out. It'll get easier."

"Yeah. I'm sure it will. I'll talk to him."

"He's reading," Jenny said. "And enthusiastic. Those are great things. A worm here or there is nothing much."

Dave brightened and got to his feet, returning the chair to its proper place. "You've got too soft a heart, Jenny. If I'd seen Jimmy do that, he'd be watching *Fear Factor* reruns for a week to see what can happen when you play with worms."

"You are one unconventional father," Jenny said, laughing. "I can see where Jimmy gets his creativity from."

Yeah, not to mention his creativity with words around women, Nate wanted to add.

"Well, it was nice to see you again, Nate. Look me up while you're in town. We'll go shoot some pool." Dave gave him a handshake. "I'm still in the book." With a final wave, Dave left.

Jenny dipped her head to study her menu. "Imagine him saying that about us being together again."

"Yeah, that's a crazy idea."

"Insane."

"So," Nate said, toying with his straw. "You seeing anyone?"

"We are *not* having this conversation."

"Why not?"

She lowered the menu and met his gaze head-on. "Because I've been down that road with you once before, Nate. I know all the bumps and all the scenic views. I also know the cliff waiting for me at the end."

"You're exaggerating."

"Am I? Oh, I forgot. You weren't here after we broke up. You didn't see how it affected me. You weren't here when my father died. You weren't here at all. That was half the problem, Nate. I was dating a ghost."

"I tried, Jenny."

She bit her lip and laid her hands flat on the menu. "We're working together this week. That's all. Then you can go back to shooting guns and taking out bad guys. And I'm going to go back to teaching kids to read. We're on different planets, Nate. Always have been. Let's just leave the past where it is, agree that we have a few good memories between us and . . . make it through this week."

It seemed as if everything in Marge's Diner had come to a halt. Jenny's words hung there in the air between them, waiting for Nate to accept them. That's what he should do.

But following orders, especially when he had a good instinct about something, had never been his strong suit. Nate was the risk taker, the first one into the battle, the one the CO pulled his hair out over, then ended up pinning a medal on when the smoke cleared.

"I have a science project for you," Nate said. The words left his mouth before he could take them back. "You and me. Again."

Chapter Five

★ ★ ★

Jenny had never eaten a piece of chicken so fast in her life. Once Nate dropped the relationship bomb on the table, she knew the dinner had been a mistake. What had she been thinking? That he'd asked her out for a friendly little conversation?

The worst part was that she'd considered his proposal for half a minute. Maybe even a full minute. Then she'd come to her senses, turned him down flat and ordered a dish of chicken parmigiana. As if everything should go right back to normal with a little mozzarella cheese and tomato sauce on top.

"What about launching rockets?" Nate said after a long moment of uncomfortable silence passed between them.

She looked into his chocolate eyes and thought he'd already done that — with his words and his mere presence. She didn't need any more of those. Not today. "Rockets?"

"For your science lesson. Me and the guys, we used to do it for kicks when things got slow on the base."

"I don't think Dr. Davis would want us lighting fires on the front lawn."

"Oh, you don't need any matches or anything. Just a film canister, an Alka Seltzer tablet and some water."

"Really? And it makes a rocket?"

"Yep. Nice demonstration of the laws of motion, too."

Jenny cupped her chin in her hands. "The kids would love it, but we're studying animal behavior in science and how the human body works in health this month. I'm not quite sure rockets fit in there."

Nate chewed, thought for a minute. "Then let's Heimlich."

"Heimlich?"

"Yeah. It's something everyone should know. Plus, you have that fake torso in your room. We could use that for a great health demonstration."

She sipped at her water, avoiding his gaze and the hypnotic effect the memory of those eyes could have on her. She was here to focus on her classroom. On Nate helping in her classroom. Nothing else. "That could work."

"Good."

She pushed her empty plate to the side. If Nate wanted to make her life and her days more distracting, she was going to do a little of that to him, too. Turnabout was fair — and necessary if she was going to keep her mind on work over the next few days. "And since you know it so well, you can teach it."

"Me? But —"

"You are trained and certified in it, right?"

"Yeah, of course."

"Then you're perfect. The kids will get to see a hero being a hero."

A shadow passed over his face and then, a second later, it was gone. He didn't say anything further, just attacked his roast beef as if it was the last meal he was ever going to eat.

"I still need a science project for Friday," Jenny said, introducing any topic other than them getting back together.

Nate pushed his plate to the side. "The kids have already responded well to animals. Why not —"

She put up her hands. "No way. I'm not bringing in Reginald or Miss BoJangles again."

"There might be something else you can do with animals that would be fun and less . . . large," Nate said.

Jenny shook her head. "I've learned my lesson there. Animals are way too unpredictable. It's like begging for pandemonium."

"A little crazy isn't bad, Jenny."

She bit her lip and caught his gaze. "Sometimes a little is too much."

Jodie came by and started to ask about dessert. She took one look at their faces, then cut off the sentence, dropped off the bill and, with a sympathetic smile at Jenny, backed away.

Small-town life. Neighbors who understood every nuance, who knew when to offer a hand and when it was best to keep quiet. Jenny loved that sense of community, that blanket that had folded around her for most of her life.

Nate tossed a twenty on the bill before she could even reach for her purse. "Nate, this isn't a date. Let me pay my half."

"Just because I pick up the tab doesn't make it a date," he said. "And even if it did, is that so bad?"

She took in a breath and shook her head. "Nate . . ."

"Yeah, I know. I'm stubborn that way." He grinned.

She didn't return the smile. Instead, she

rose, grabbing her purse from the booth and leaving a ten on the table out of principle — and to send a message to him and to herself that dating was out of the question. One heartbreak in a lifetime was enough. "I'll see you in the morning."

"You don't want to go for a walk in the park? It was part of my promised evening."

She knew where that would lead. She'd already stretched her resolve to its breaking point, sitting three feet across from him, trying not to think about what it would be like to have his lips on hers again, to feel those strong, capable arms around her. "Sorry, no. Lewis and Clark are waiting for me."

He opened his mouth to say something, though better of it, and nodded. "Tomorrow morning it is then. Me, you and Mr. Body."

Jenny turned and left Marge's Diner before her resolve could overpower her feet and make her turn back.

Nate saw Jenny go and knew he should let her leave. It would be best — for both of them.

But damned if the sight of her leaving didn't undo all his best intentions and have him up and out of the seat, hurrying after her as best he could with the silly cane and his stupid, recalcitrant knee.

He reached the sidewalk just a few seconds after she did. "Jenny!"

She turned around and stopped on the sidewalk. Good thing because he sure as heck wasn't up to running after her. Six months ago, he could have taken on the Boston Marathon without a lot of trouble. Today, a toddler could beat him in a sack race.

"Don't leave yet. Let's talk."

Her mouth curved into a smile that seemed more sad than anything else. "We did, Nate. You know my answer. It's not going to change." She took a few steps forward, meeting him where he stood. "We had a nice thing a long time ago. Let's just leave it there. A memory."

No, he wanted to scream. He didn't want the memory. He wanted the real thing. He wanted Jenny, back in his arms, back in his bed, back in his life.

But to get that, he knew what he needed to do. He had to say the five words that he had yet to get past his voice box. *I'm not a marine anymore.*

Every inch of him still felt like one. The thought of adventure still quickened in his veins. How could he explain that to her?

91

And how could he expect her to invite him back into her life when he didn't want the small-town, confining life she'd chosen?

Just then, Miss Marchand came down the sidewalk, right toward Jenny and by extension, Nate. Her little dog trotted at her side, on the end of a fancy leash with rhinestones running the length of it. "Why, Jenny Wright and Nate Dole," she said when she spied them. "Fancy seeing you two here. And together."

"We're not —" Jenny began.

"Nice to see you, Miss Marchand," Nate interrupted. Whether he could have Jenny or not, he was tired of hearing her tell everyone they weren't together. That particular nail had been driven home enough today. It was a continual reminder that he couldn't have what he wanted. "It's been a long time since I last saw you."

Miss Marchand looked the same as always. An imposing woman despite her age, Miss Marchand's bearing stood in sharp contrast to her loose-fitting floral dress and short curly gray hair. A plump woman, she looked as if she could be someone's grandmother, though as far as Nate knew, she'd never married. Probably because Miss Marchand expected a great deal out of everyone she met.

Miss Marchand pointed a finger at him. "You, young man, don't come home often enough. Worry your poor mother half to death, traipsing all over the world."

"I'm home now, for a while." For as long as he could stand Mercy and figure out what the hell kind of career possibilities there were for a former war machine with one good working leg.

"Well, good." Miss Marchand looked to Jenny, then to Nate. "You know, you're the only Dole child who is unmarried. Seems I haven't set my sights on you yet."

"Set your sights?" He looked at this former biology teacher, who had to be close to eighty by now. He hoped she wasn't thinking what she seemed to be implying. Undoubtedly, Miss Marchand could run faster than he could; she'd nab him before he could get away.

"I had a hand in all your brothers' and your sister's happy endings, don't you know. I'm not butting my nose in or anything, but I do like to call a spade out when I see one." She smiled at Jenny. "Or a heart or a diamond, whatever the case may be."

Miss Marchand couldn't have dropped a bigger hint-hint about marriage if she tried. Beside him, Nate saw Jenny blanch, then swallow and recover her composure.

"Miss Marchand, you must be playing a lot of euchre lately," Jenny said, her face bright and clearly determined to change the subject. "How are you and Miss Tanner doing in the Mercy Euchre Club? Beating everyone?"

"Don't you try and change the subject now. I'm an old woman, but not a stupid one." She bent down toward her little dog. "Isn't that right, Sugarplum?"

The dachshund gave a little yip in response.

Miss Marchand returned her attention to Nate. "I hope while you're home, young man, you revisit some of your favorite haunts *and* bring back some of those old memories." She cast a hinting glance Jenny's way, before bidding them a good night and continuing on her way with her dachshund trotting alongside.

Seemed half the town wanted him and Jenny back together. That was the trouble with small towns. They liked to butt in on personal business and make it their own. If people thought they could fashion a happy marriage out of two loose ends, they would.

Of course, they only knew half the story. They hadn't been there for the breakup;

they didn't know what had happened to Nate in the past few months. As far as Nate knew, Jenny could even be dating someone.

But she hadn't protested Miss Marchand's obvious romantic machinations. If he were smart, he'd take that as a good sign. Of what?

Of a future between them?

Hell, if he were honest with himself, he knew that if it were possible, he'd have Jenny back in his life in an instant. Wanting her had never been the problem.

Keeping her — and meshing their opposite worlds — had.

"I think I need to find Miss Marchand a new hobby," Jenny said after the woman had gone. "She's been running around town with Miss Tanner like Mercy's version of a one-on-one matchmaking service."

The two of them started back toward the school parking lot. "Maybe the Misses have something there. I hear Miss Tanner had a hand in Mark and Claire's relationship, from what Mark told me."

"What she needs is someone matchmaking in *her* life. Then she'll leave other people's alone."

"Is it so bad?" Nate asked. "Her wanting

to see you happily married and with a few kids?"

She turned toward him, that emerald gaze connecting with his, her eyes full of honesty and seeking the same in return. "There's nothing wrong with that. The only problem, as I see it, is Miss Marchand's choice. You were never really much for that kind of thing, Nate. White picket fences keep you hemmed in, remember?"

He'd said those words to her once, a long time ago. He winced to think of them now. But they were true. The thought of being in one place forever — particularly this small place — made him claustrophobic. It was why he'd joined the marines, traveled the world, never had more than a few weeks or months in any one place. "Yeah, that's me. Made for the open range."

"Well, it works out in the end, then. Since we're not dating, you have all the space you want with me. *Except* when you're in my classroom." She grinned, clearly making an attempt at changing the tone from serious to light-hearted. "Then you're all mine from eight-thirty to three every day."

Her smile, that beautiful angelic smile he'd never been able to resist, brought a mirroring one to his own face and pushed the darker thoughts out of his mind. "Do with me what you will, Miss Wright, but just don't make me eat worms."

She wagged a finger at him, a tease in her eyes. "Behave yourself, Nate Dole, and we'll get along just fine."

On the surface, Nate knew it looked like everything was just fine between them again. Yet, something unfinished lingered in the air, telling him he might not want the white-picket-fence life, but he wasn't over wanting Jenny.

Not by a long shot.

Jenny arrived a half hour earlier than normal on Tuesday morning, more to get her bearings before Nate came in than anything else. She'd barely slept the night before and ended up blazing through the rest of her week's work in the wee hours of the morning.

The good news was that she was ahead for the first time in weeks. The bad news? She had nothing to occupy herself after school today. And tomorrow. And all the tomorrows after that when Nate's reentry into her life would still be lingering in her heart.

"Miss Wright?"

Jenny looked up from the pile of papers on her desk. "Jimmy. What are you doing here so early?"

"My mom dropped me off again. She said you wouldn't mind."

Jenny thought of what might have happened had she not come in early this morning. The building had been pretty empty when she arrived, and Jimmy would have waited in the hall. Alone. She wondered, not for the first time, what had happened in Dave and Kim's marriage.

Not to mention what on earth Kim was thinking lately.

"Did your mom have to go to work early?"

Jimmy made a sour look. "She's meeting someone. Some guy. She says she loves him. Wants to make him my new dad."

Jenny's heart ached for the little boy in front of her, the cowlick that made his hair forever fall into a scoop over his eyes, the big blue eyes that had seen and been through so much in nine years.

Jimmy started to fidget, as if the scrutiny was too much.

"You want to help me put out the morning work?" she asked.

"Sure!" He zipped off, dumped his book bag and coat in the coat closet, then ran back to her desk. Jenny handed him a stack of spelling worksheets and he took off, weaving in and out of the desks and dropping the papers like little bombs on each desk.

Dr. Davis poked her head in the room. "Miss Wright, may I see you? Now?"

"Certainly." Jenny turned to the whirling dervish scooting around her room. "Jimmy, you can start your paper when you're done handing the others out."

Jenny joined the principal in the quiet hallway. Dr. Davis swallowed. She played with the glasses on the chain around her neck. "You don't have any animals on your agenda today, do you?"

"Me? No. Just an ordinary day in third grade."

"Well, your version of ordinary and mine are quite different," Dr. Davis said. "Be that as it may, I need you to help me today."

"Help you?" Two times in the space of a week, the principal had come to her looking for help. There definitely had to be something in the air. Maybe Mercy needed to check its smog level because Dr. Davis wasn't thinking straight.

"One of the members of the state accreditation board, Howard Perkins, is coming by today to observe your classroom. Apparently he saw this." Dr. Davis held up that morning's *Mercy Daily News.* Splashed across the front page were two pictures. One of Jenny about to kiss the fainting goat, the other of she and Dr. Davis standing together in the hall with the farmer from Animals Where You Want 'Em off to the side. "He's . . . concerned."

Oh, Lord. Not again. Damn that farmer and his penchant for publicity. "Dr. Davis. I had no idea that guy was going to come in here with that goat. I —"

"It doesn't matter. If they think we're running a zoo out of this school," she swung her glasses on the chain again, "I don't know what they'll do." Dr. Davis drew in a breath and seemed to refocus herself. "Please run your classroom efficiently and professionally today. And for God's sake, whatever you do, don't go unconventional on me."

Dr. Davis turned on her heel and walked away, her back stiff and her concerns clear in the heavy set of her shoulders.

Jenny returned to the classroom and began to put a plan into action. Nothing would get off course today. Nothing would run late. If anything went wrong, it would undoubtedly mean her job.

And that was a risk — just like the risk of getting close to Nate again — that she wasn't going to take.

Chapter Six

★ ★ ★

Nate headed into Mercy Elementary School at the exact same time as he had the day before, surprising himself that he'd actually made it here. Today, he'd opted to walk the five or so blocks from his house to the school as penance for his indecision this morning.

Ever since enemy fire had taken out both his knee and his career at the same time, Nate had found it easier to avoid than confront. When he'd been a marine, he'd been the exact opposite, but now, without his uniform on, it was as if he'd lost the part of himself that knew how to battle.

He'd wavered for twenty minutes this morning, standing there in his cluttered kitchen, holding a cup of coffee and thinking how much easier it would be just to go back to the couch and not face Jenny, the classroom, or hell, the world again. Then he'd glanced at his counter and seen the "prescription" from his doctor.

A week with Jenny would do him good, his doctor had said. Well, it might, but it also opened up a barrel of problems bigger than he'd anticipated.

Again, he'd looked from one destination to the other — the sofa, then the note. Then he'd had a good long lecture with himself, becoming his own worst drill instructor.

Enough of the self-pity. Enough of the woe-is-me-with-the-bad-knee crap. It was time for him to get over it, get out and do something about the situation he found himself in.

He wasn't going back to the marines. But he still needed to eat and live, so he better damned well find something to do with himself — and soon. First thing on his list was Jenny's class, whether she wanted him there or not.

In the end, he was here. And his sofa sat empty for a second day.

"Mr. Dole! You're here again today?" Alex Herman came running up to him, accompanying him on the walk from the front door down to Jenny's class.

When Nate looked over at the boy, he was struck by the height difference between them. Clearly, he'd been working with adults for too long. The kid looked like a ranch house next to a skyscraper. "Yes, I am. Remember, I'm Miss Wright's helper this week."

"Can you tell us how machine guns work and how you blow up all the bad guys today?"

"Uh, no. That's really not appropriate for a third-grade classroom."

"Oh, okay." Alex walked for a minute, then looked up again at Nate. "You sure?"

Nate chuckled. "Yeah, I'm sure."

He thought of himself at that age, and of his childhood fascination with cops, firemen and GI Joes. If he'd met a real marine at that age, he would have been all over the guy, just as the boys in Jenny's class were, to tell him something — anything — about what it was like. Gory details and all.

"All right." Nate smiled, relenting a little. "If you're good today and do all your work, I'll tell you a few of my stories from the marines at the end of the day, as long as it's okay with Miss Wright." The cleaner, tamer, G-rated stories at least.

At this point, Nate wasn't even sure if it was okay with Miss Wright that *he* was here, never mind sharing any tales of military life. But he'd cross that bridge when he got to it.

He halted just inside the door of her room. She was bent over her desk, her hair tucked behind her ears again, dressed in a long, light-blue dress that made her seem almost angelic. He'd screwed up yesterday by pushing her too hard, by thinking he could have back the one thing he'd lost.

Whether he'd decided to get off his pity couch or not, that didn't change things between himself and Jenny. She'd made that clear last night and he knew, if he pushed her too hard, he'd only push her away. He'd be best off remembering that and sticking to the task at hand.

He noticed Jimmy at the front of the room, rearranging the books in the reading circle.

"Have I been replaced?" Nate joked, heading into the room. His knee was still throbbing from all the activity yesterday and the walk this morning, but he forced himself not to wince as he made the final steps toward a desk where he could take a seat.

Jenny's head jerked up and she turned toward him. "Nate. You're here."

"As promised."

"I wasn't sure . . ."

"I keep my promises, Jenny." *Now,* he wanted to add. *Now I keep my promises.*

Because he didn't have anything else to do but keep them.

Alex had dropped off his stuff and was already front and center, eager to help, too. Jenny gave him a sheaf of corrected papers to stick into his classmates' folders, then gestured to Nate. "Mr. Dole, can I talk to you for a minute, before the class gets here?"

"Certainly." They left the boys working on their tasks and went out into the hall. Around them, the buzz of morning activity had already started as children made their way down the hall to their homerooms.

"I want to talk to you about today." She tucked her hair behind her ear and took in a breath. He knew, from the movement, that she was nervous. Because of him? Or something else? "There's a member of the accreditation board coming here today to observe my classroom and a few others. I need everything to be perfect."

"As perfect as things can be in third grade."

"That means no funny business." She eyed him.

"You can trust me. Here at least."

Jenny let out a breath and bit her lip. "That's another thing I wanted to talk to you about. Last night —"

"Don't," he said. "Don't say it again."

"I think it needs to be said, don't you? I can see it in your eyes. You still want to try that 'experiment' of us dating again."

"And what's wrong with that?" He lowered his voice as the hall began to fill with children. "Are you telling me you aren't interested in me anymore? Not at all?"

"No." But she looked away when she said the word.

"Liar."

"Do you remember why we broke up, Nate?" Her voice was low, too, nearly a whisper in the humming, busy hallway. "Because we were from totally different worlds. We wanted completely different things. If you can tell me that's changed, that you want to settle down in Mercy and make this your life, then maybe I'll change my mind."

He leaned against the wall, crossing his arms over his chest and giving his knee a break. "Or maybe you've just made up that little condition because you're afraid."

"Me? Afraid? Of what?"

"Of getting involved. With me. Or anyone else. You're not married. Or divorced. Or dating anyone that I know of. That tells me you've either become a recluse or you're afraid of getting involved."

She frowned. "This is neither the time nor the place to discuss this."

"I agree. So let's pick a time — when we can be alone."

She shook her head. "Persistent, aren't you?"

He grinned. "My mother always said it should have been my middle name."

A trio of girls came chattering past them and into the room. They greeted Jenny and Nate, then headed into the coat closet to hang up their things. "I have to get back to my class," Jenny said, turning to reenter the room.

"Later, Jenny, we *will* talk about this."

"All I want to concentrate on is getting through today. My class is the most important thing right now."

He wanted to ask why — why she was using that as a wall every time he got close, but he didn't have time. The bell was ringing and the kids were streaming in. The day was beginning, and he had another six and a half hours with two dozen chaperones before he could have Jenny to himself again.

Two hours later, Nate and Jenny were at the front of the room again, this time accompanied by Mr. Body. As promised,

Howard Perkins, the board member from the accreditation committee, had arrived a few minutes earlier and taken a seat in the back of the room. He'd spread out a notebook, readied a mechanical pencil and sat back, waiting for Jenny to conduct her class.

She cast a nervous glance back at Mr. Perkins, then returned her attention to her students. "Today, children, for our health lesson on the human body, we're going to learn about the Heimlich maneuver."

"Heimlich?" Lindsay screwed up her face. "Is that like that Einstein guy you told us about? He was boring. And he had that crazy haircut, too."

Jenny laughed. "No, not like Einstein. The Heimlich maneuver is a lifesaving technique that you do to someone who is choking."

Alex poked his hand into the air and started talking before Jenny acknowledged him. "Like when my sister had a big piece of candy and we had to call the paramedics and they came and —"

"Alex, remember we have to take turns when we want to talk. And wait to be called on before starting." Jenny cast a glance toward the suit in the back of the room. "Let's share at the *end* of the lesson, shall we?" She gestured toward Nate.

"Now, since Mr. Dole is certified in the Heimlich maneuver and CPR as part of his military training, he's going to demonstrate this for us today."

"On who?" Jimmy asked. "On that guy in the back of the room?"

Mr. Perkins popped his head up and for a second, looked worried.

Jenny cleared her throat. "Ah, no. On Mr. Body."

"Mr. Body?" Jimmy gave the plastic anatomy figure a dubious glance. "But he's fake. That's no fun. He can't even really eat. Or choke."

"Our goal here, Jimmy, isn't to have anyone come close to dying."

"Sure would be a lot cooler if you did. We could get that Rescue 911 TV show in here and —"

"Jimmy, get out your health notebook, please."

Jimmy pouted. "Yes, ma'am."

Jenny cast a glance at the clock, then signaled to Nate. "Time to get started. We have just enough time for this before morning recess." Jenny hoisted the plastic torso off the table beside her and placed it on the smaller desk in front of Nate. "Mr. Dole, meet Mr. Body."

Nate put out his hand and pretended to

shake the nonexistent hand of the faux man, who had all his organs exposed for demonstration purposes. "Pleasure to meet you. You're looking a little transparent today, sir."

The kids roared with laughter. Jenny gave him a look that begged him not to make the class too fun, lest Mr. Perkins find fun offensive.

"All right, kids." Nate stood and moved behind Mr. Body. "Let's say Mr. Body has just gotten one really big chicken nugget. And he didn't bother to chew it before trying to swallow."

The kids snickered.

"So now that chicken nugget, it's squawking in Mr. Body's esophagus." Nate pointed to the front of Mr. Body's neck. "And now, we have to get it out."

"Or Mr. Body's going to be one dead body," Jimmy piped up.

Nate bit back a grin. "The first thing you need to do is get behind the victim who is choking. Put your right hand underneath their sternum. That's this bone right here." Nate demonstrated. "Then take your left hand and lock it over your right wrist. Then you thrust upward. Like so." Nate gave Mr. Body a lifesaving thrust.

Mr. Body responded by regurgitating

more than just an imaginary chicken nugget. Kidneys, liver, heart, lungs — they all went flying across the room in a shower of demonstrable body parts.

The pancreas spiraled up and over the students' heads and conked Mr. Perkins on the right temple. He jerked back, dropped his pencil and blinked in surprise, rubbing at the dent left by the errant organ.

"Guess I won't be on Mr. Body's list of friends to call when he needs a lifeline, huh?" Nate said.

That only made the kids laugh harder. Nate glanced over at Jenny.

She glared back. Apparently she wasn't very thrilled with the idea of a pair of kidneys on her floor.

Across the room, Nate heard the visitor's pencil scratching across his pad. Clearly, he was making a note of the event. The look on his face said he hadn't been too thrilled about Nate's overzealous Heimliching Harry event.

The children, however, were still laughing. Nate had a fan club of twenty-five in the room.

And two who would probably be glad to see him gone.

Nate figured he'd start with retrieving Mr. Body's liver. Then he'd set to work on trying to get Jenny's heart back in the right place, too.

By the time the kidneys were back in Mr. Body, Jenny could see the writing on the board. Her career was going to go down in a mess of discarded body parts and loose intestines. Howard Perkins had a sour look on his face and a long list of notes on his pad. All bad signs.

She glanced at the clock. "Time for morning recess," she said. "Everyone get on your coats, in table order, and line up to go out."

The children, still laughing at the Heimlich disaster, did as they were told with minimal shoving. Perkins followed the children outside, taking a seat on one of the benches under an elm tree, the ubiquitous notebook by his side.

"I'm sorry about the disemboweling earlier," Nate said once they were outside. "That's not the normal result of the Heimlich maneuver."

She let out a sigh. "This is not going well. If another thing goes wrong —"

"Jenny, this is third grade. Things go wrong. You can't expect perfection. You know that, I'm sure."

She wheeled around to face him. "On

any other day, fine. But today, there's a lot at stake. My job, the school —"

"You worry too much. This was a small thing. It wasn't the end of the world. Mr. Perkins isn't going to recommend pulling accreditation just because Mr. Body up-chucked his organs."

She bit her lip, and he knew she wanted to disagree but wouldn't because the kids were all around them and Mr. Perkins was watching from his perch across the way.

"Why do you have to keep such a tight leash on everything, Jenny?"

The tension between them sat in stark contrast to the bright, laughing world of the playground. "Since when did it become okay for you to come back into my world and start questioning my life?"

He paused a moment, taking in the halo of hair around her face. "Tell me this . . . when have I ever been out of your world?"

In her eyes, in the hitch in her breath, he saw and heard the truth. Never. She hadn't forgotten the years they'd spent together, the kisses they'd shared. The dreams they'd whispered to each other in the back seat of his Grand Am, parked behind the old Emery Farm property.

She hadn't forgotten and God forgive him, neither had he.

"I — I — I better go stop Jimmy. Seems he's got his hands on some bugs." In a flash, Jenny was gone, across the playground and about as far away from him as she could get in the schoolyard.

From where he was, Nate saw Jimmy presenting his insect treasure to Lindsay at the same time Alex came up and thrust himself between the two. The two boys exchanged a few words, with each casting glances at the pretty brunette.

Then, before Jenny reached them, the first punch was thrown.

Jenny broke into a run. Nate did, too. Not the best run but one nonetheless. He skidded to a stop beside the fighting boys a second after she did.

"Stop it!" Jenny said, trying to pull the boys off one another. They ignored her, continuing their battle. Jimmy swung wildly at Alex, his face streaked with tears, hitting at anything in his path.

Nate knew the powerhouse of double nine-year-old male energy was too much for Jenny. He inserted himself into the scuffle and pulled the boys apart before one of them hurt the other really badly or worse, hit Jenny. "Hey, hey. Let's not fight."

"He started it," they both huffed out,

trying to catch their breath and still look like the victor.

"What was this about?" Jenny said, hands on her hips. "You know fighting is against the rules."

"I wanted to show Lindsay the bug."

"And I wanted to show Lindsay my new sneakers. You got in the way." Alex sent Jimmy an angry look.

"Well, Lindsay is already off playing with Josey. Apparently you two fighting made her lose interest in the bug *and* the sneakers," Jenny said. "Now there's nothing to fight over. And I want both of you to serve detention tomorrow."

"But, Miss Wright!"

"No buts. You know the rules."

Alex nodded, accepting his punishment, and went off in the direction of the swings.

Jimmy kept the chip on his shoulder and scowled. "I bet Mr. Dole would fight for a girl he liked. He wouldn't let her go with some other guy." He glanced up at Nate. "Wouldn't you fight? Isn't that what marines do?"

Nate swallowed. "Well, yeah, we do, Jimmy, but there are rules for marines, too."

"Rules are stupid," Jimmy muttered. "All they do is get you in trouble."

Nate exchanged a glance with Jenny. He had to bite back his laugh, but he didn't see an answering sense of humor in Jenny. He saw too much of himself in Jimmy, and he was willing to bet Jenny did, too. That was probably why she didn't think it was funny.

Across the playground, Hannah fell off a swing and started to cry. Jenny's face shifted into concern. "Go," Nate said. "I'll handle this."

"Are you sure?"

"Yeah. We speak the same language, Jimmy and me."

Worry about that particular alliance crossed her features, but Hannah's potential injuries won out and Jenny dashed over to the little girl.

Nate waved toward a big rock that sat to the left of the playground equipment, shaded by a big maple tree. "Let's go over here and talk for a few minutes."

Jimmy nodded and the two of them took a seat on the hard, flat surface. Around them, the playground was a noisy whirlwind of activity and shouts as the kids started up an impromptu kickball game, made good use of the playground equipment or just played a rousing game of tag.

"You know, Jimmy, when I was a kid,"

Nate said, "I was a lot like you."

"You were?"

"Yeah. I wanted to be the hero. I wanted to win all the battles, take on everyone who thought they were bigger than me."

"Did you? And did you win?"

"I took most of them on, but then Ricky Lincoln came along."

"Who was he?"

"Someone who taught me a very important lesson." Nate draped his arms over his knees and for a second, turned his face up to the sun and enjoyed the moment in the spring air. Just as Jenny would have. A feeling of peace stole over him, something he hadn't felt in a long, long time.

After a minute, Nate returned his attention to the little boy beside him. "When I was ten, I wanted a new bike more than anything in the world. I *had* a bike, but it was a hand-me-down from my older brother. What I really wanted was a bike of my own. Money was tight for my mom and dad because there were five of us, so my dad and I cut a deal. I'd save up half the money and he'd kick in the rest."

"You had to work for something you wanted?" Jimmy shook his head. "Man. My mom always buys me whatever I ask for."

"I'll tell you something, Jimmy, when you work for something of your own, you feel really proud. I earned that money and I bought that bike and whenever I rode it, I felt like a superhero."

"Really?"

"Yep. Because *I* bought and paid for it. It made me feel like I could do anything."

"Huh." Nate could see Jimmy turning that over in his mind. "Was that it? New bike, happy ending?"

"Not exactly. First day I was out in the neighborhood, riding my new bike around, and who came up but Ricky Lincoln. He was bigger than me. And stronger. And he wanted that bike."

"Why?"

"Because I had a new one and he didn't."

Jimmy's eyes were wide with interest. He was hooked on Nate's story, as caught up in the telling as a reader of a great book. He had scooted closer, his body turned to face Nate's. "So what happened?"

"He and I got into a fight. I was beating him, even though he was bigger. I was a pretty tough kid. Guess I watched too many Bruce Lee movies when I was little." He grinned, saw the blank look on Jimmy's face and added a bit of explanation. "He was like Jackie Chan."

"Oh, yeah. Jackie's cool."

"Anyway, Ricky started to cry. That had never happened before when I'd been in a fight. Granted, I hadn't been in a lot of them as a kid, but never had I seen anybody cry. I didn't know what to do, so I stopped fighting. I just kind of stared at him."

"Did he beat you up after that?"

"No. He kind of . . . gave up." Nate remembered how Ricky had seemed to shrink into himself, like he'd left a part of his strength on the ground with the fallen tears. "I felt bad. Really bad. So I asked him what was wrong. If I'd hurt him or something."

"And what'd he say?"

"It took him a while, because he was this big tough guy and telling the truth wasn't something Ricky did often. But after a while, he told me he wanted my bike because he didn't have one at all. In fact, he'd never even ridden a bike. Ever."

"Ever in his whole life?"

"Yeah. His parents were really poor and couldn't afford one either. But Ricky, he was the strong guy around school, and he wasn't going to let anyone know that. So he decided to try to get one by using the only thing he had — his fists."

"And when it didn't work, he gave up?"

"Yeah, but giving up kind of changed something in him, too. Made him more like me, I guess." Nate drew in a breath, his mind running back over those images from almost two decades before. "I told him how I'd saved up for mine by doing odd jobs and mowing lawns and stuff like that. And I offered to help him do the same."

"Why?" Jimmy's eyes grew wide. "I mean, he just wanted to beat your face in five minutes before that."

"Because I knew how he felt. I knew what it was like to want something that you couldn't have." Nate noticed Jenny had finished with Hannah and was standing off to the side, listening in on their conversation, a bemused — and slightly surprised — smile on her face. "And that summer, I taught Ricky how to ride a bike — my bike — until he had enough money to buy his own."

"You did? But weren't you worried he'd steal it?"

"Sometimes, Jimmy, you have to trust people. Even if they've done bad things before, sometimes they can change."

Jimmy shook his head. "I don't know if I could do that."

"Sure you can. You have a built in truth-o-meter, you know."

Jimmy raised a doubtful brow.

"Everything you need to know about what to do and when to do it is in here," Nate said, pressing a hand to his abdomen. "All the right answers are there. In your gut. Listen to it and it will tell you when to trust someone and when not to, when to make up and when to fight."

Jimmy was quiet for a long time, digesting those words. "Maybe I should tell Alex I'm sorry," he said finally, looking across the playground at his former combatant, now toeing at the ground from a seat on a swing.

"Sounds like a good start to me."

Jimmy let out a breath, then heaved himself up to his feet, seeming older than his nine years. "I wish all grown-ups were as smart as you, Mr. Dole." Then he ran off, without explaining what he meant.

Jenny came over and took a seat on the rock beside him, smoothing the skirt of her pale-blue dress beneath her as she did. In the sun, she looked younger, almost like the girl he'd known in high school. When they'd been kids, they'd sat on this exact rock once and debated whether Mallomars were better than Three Musketeers bars.

As Nate remembered it, Mallomars won, hands down.

"I never heard you tell that story before," Jenny said.

"It's not one I tell. When I was a kid, keeping Ricky's reputation intact was more important, at least to him." He grinned.

"I remember you guys being friends when we were kids. You were such opposites, it seemed so unusual."

Nate shrugged. "Now you know why."

She cocked her head and studied him. "You surprise me, Nate. I never dreamed there was anything about you I didn't know."

"There's a lot, Jenny. A whole lot." More than he would get into now, on this big rock in the middle of the Mercy Elementary playground. But someday, if she'd give him a chance, he wanted to tell her.

She opened her mouth to ask him something else, but was cut off by another third-grade calamity.

"Miss Wright! Cole pushed me!" called one of the kids from the kickball game.

"That's my cue to get back to work." She glanced at her watch. "And it's time to go back in."

He reached for her hand before she could run off. "Wait, just for one second."

She glanced over her shoulder, saw the kids had remedied their own situation, and turned back to him. "Okay. One."

"What I told Jimmy is true. Sometimes you have to trust your instincts with people. No matter who they were before, you can give them a second chance."

Around them, the busy world of third grade went on, filled with shouts and laughter. The birds called to each other from the trees, seemingly annoyed that the tranquility of their homes was being disturbed by young voices. The world went on, oblivious to an old love that one was trying to rekindle and another kept blowing out.

Jenny clasped her palm over their joined hands, the touch both warm and inviting, as if they'd made a connection. A flare of hope rose in his chest. Then she let go and stepped back, doubt filling her green eyes. "*Have* you changed, Nate? Or are you still going to leave this place in your dust and rush off to the far corners of the world, always the superhero?"

He didn't know the answer to that. He knew he couldn't go back to who he was before. But he didn't know who — or what — he was going to become now. "I don't know, Jenny. I can't make you any guarantees right now."

"Then my gut is saying not to take a chance on something I can't count on." She gave him a quick, sad smile, then left him.

Alone, on a rock. He couldn't have picked a better metaphor for his life right now if he tried.

Well, hell.

Nate got to his feet, grabbed his cane and decided he'd had just enough of that. The self-pity fest was over. He sure as hell wanted to feel like a superhero again. In his heart . . .

And in Jenny's eyes.

Chapter Seven

★ ★ ★

Nate had been right. Boy, did Jenny hate to admit it.

Mr. Perkins had actually found a little humor in the pancreas dive-bombing his temple. "Miss Wright, I think your class, though unconventional, has some merit," Howard Perkins said after the morning recess. The children had their heads buried in a math worksheet and Nate was busy setting up for that day's history lesson. Jenny and Mr. Perkins were standing off to the side, reviewing his notes from the Heimlich disaster. "That said," Mr. Perkins continued, "I'm concerned about the recent public events involving yourself and your classroom. That, coupled with the low reading scores, has me concerned that Mercy Elementary is worried too much about having fun and not enough about education."

"I assure you, Mr. Perkins, we are very committed to education. A lot of the fun things we've done have been incentives for the kids."

"A Tennessee Fainting Goat as an incentive?"

"That was an . . . accident. And, the goat won't be returning."

That seemed to reassure him. He gave her a nod and pushed his glasses up on his nose. "Glad to hear it. Though I do hope you can focus on more serious matters from here on out." He walked back to his chosen seat, again opening the notebook and clicking a new lead into his pencil.

Nate raised a brow at Jenny. She gave him a shrug that said she wasn't sure if things were going well . . . or worse. He sent her a surreptitious thumbs-up, then crossed to Mr. Perkins.

Oh no, Jenny thought. Here came Nate again to the rescue. She did not need him interfering, not when she'd just straightened everything out.

"Mr. Perkins, why don't you try something with the children today?" Nate said, placing a hand on the man's back and easing him up and out of his chair. "I'm sure they'd love to have another participating guest."

"Mr. Dole," Jenny said, laying the hint heavy in her voice, "I'm sure Mr. Perkins doesn't want — or need — to be involved right now. He's happy observing."

"Miss Wright is correct," the other man said, pushing his spectacles up the bridge of his nose. "I couldn't possibly —"

"Sure you could. The kids are just about to start their history lesson for today."

"What are you doing?" Jenny mouthed to Nate, giving him a pointed look that told him she didn't want him butting into her classroom again. Short of dragging him out of the room like an errant puppy, though, there was no real way to stop him. She had a feeling serving Nate with a detention wouldn't be much of a deterrent.

Nate gave Jenny a grin and a confident look that told her to trust him. That was the whole problem. Trusting Nate.

And yet, he had been a good addition to the classroom thus far. He'd worked wonders with Jimmy earlier. He'd enthralled the kids with his reading and his presence. Thus far, he hadn't done anything that made the situation in her classroom — or the pressures on the school to please the accreditation board — worse.

Save for the flying pancreas incident.

"Well, I always did like history," Mr. Perkins said, rubbing his chin. "What are they studying?"

Interest peaked in Mr. Perkins's eyes. For the first time that day, he cracked a smile. Maybe Nate's idea wasn't so crazy after all.

"Pompeii," Jenny said, stepping forward and joining the duo as they made their way to the front of the room. "It's part of a series we've been doing on Europe. Today, we're talking about the volcano that wiped out that city."

"Really? I like volcanoes. In fact, my undergraduate degree is in geological studies." Mr. Perkins shoved his glasses up again.

"Really?" Nate said. "That would make you the perfect leader for our volcano eruption."

"Eruption? Like . . . a reenactment?"

Jenny gestured toward a small volcano the children had made out of papier-mâché. Beneath it, they'd built a mini city from toothpicks and recycled milk cartons from lunch.

"Just like the real thing," Nate said, leading the other man toward the display. "Here, you won't need this." He laid Mr. Perkins's pad and pencil on Jenny's desk.

"What's the plan here? Blow up Mr. Perkins?" Jenny whispered, stepping back to Nate's side.

"I hadn't considered that." He laughed. "Actually, my idea is to teach your criticizer what it's like to be a teacher. And get him away from that little notebook of his for a while."

"Have I told you today how brilliant you are?"

"Not lately, but you're welcome to let loose any time you feel like it."

She gave him a little jab in the shoulder, then crossed to Mr. Perkins, who was standing over the Pompeii exhibit, ready to launch death and destruction on her cue. "The volcano has a two-liter bottle inside it. You can use a funnel to pour in the ingredients —"

"Miss Wright, I know how to make my own volcano. I do have a degree in geological studies." Mr. Perkins drew his shoulders back and thrust his chest forward, clearly now in his element. "I can mix the ingredients in the proper ratio and explain the physics behind the eruption to the children."

"It's just . . . you really need to be precise. Too much of one thing and —"

Mr. Perkins turned to her, confidence on his face. "I can handle it."

Dread sank to the pit of Jenny's stomach. Why had she agreed to this plan? If anything went wrong —

Jenny backed away to stand by Nate, both of them far enough from the volcano to save them, should Mr. Perkins get too overzealous in his recreation of the Pompeii disaster. The children, separated by an empty row from Mr. Perkins, had squirmed in their seats while the adults settled the matter and now sprang to attention to see what their previously silent guest had to say.

"First, let me begin with a history of the volcano, and the one in Pompeii in particular . . ." Mr. Perkins launched into a twenty-minute lecture on lava and magma. By the time he got to the actual eruption, the excitement of speaking on his favorite topic had him chomping at the baking soda, ready to wipe out the toothpick Pompeii.

"Be careful with the —" Jenny began.

But it was too late. Mr. Perkins, in his zeal, had quickly funneled in a mixture of vinegar, food coloring and a few drops of dish detergent, then begun spooning in the baking soda without regard to the chemical results.

Mini Mount Vesuvius took no prisoners in Jenny Wright's classroom. The faux lava bubbled up with a gushing force, spewing out of the newspaper and glue form,

131

churning down the sides in cascading pink bubbles, and falling to the floor in a spreading puddle of destruction.

"Cool!" the class shouted.

Jenny gasped and dove for the paper towels. Nate bit back a chuckle and rushed for paper reinforcements, too. Mr. Perkins, eyes wide, watched the spewing pretend lava and reiterated facts from 79 A.D. "Imagine it, children. The people were going about their daily lives when this monster hit. Pliny, the historian of that time, wrote that the earth shook and the sea swept backward, crashing back in on them with a tidal wave. It was incredible."

"You can say that again," Jenny said, keeping a smile on her face as she got up the worst of the gloopy mess with a pile of paper towels. "Class, now that you've seen what a volcano can do and how it wiped out our little city —"

"Not to mention half the desk and the floor," Jimmy added.

"— you can write an essay on what it was like to go through this, and survive it," Jenny continued. Her first priority was to restore order. Then she'd get to the mess — both the lava one and the Mr. Perkins one. "Not everyone died in Pompeii. Many made it to the boats and survived. Now, tell me your story and add in the details of the volcano."

Within seconds, all twenty-five children had paper and pencils before them. There was little sound in the room besides the busy scribbling of words.

Jenny tossed out the paper towels and took a look over her shoulder at Nate, who had finished cleaning up his half. He was grinning at her again, damn him.

"Well, that was a great deal of fun, if a bit . . . messy." Mr. Perkins looked down at his suit, no longer as pressed and neat as it had been that morning.

Nate had been right. Again. Mr. Perkins wasn't mad. He nearly glowed with joy at the experience.

"And the kids learned a lot," Jenny added, handing Mr. Perkins a damp paper towel to wipe off the worst of the lava damage. "You have a wealth of knowledge, Mr. Perkins."

He glanced at the class, still busy writing. "I'm happy to see them take such an interest in the subject."

She knew now what lesson Nate had been trying to impart when he'd turned the tables on the accreditation board member. He'd been giving Mr. Perkins a taste of Jenny medicine — without the kissing pig. She'd do well to take advantage of this and plead her case while she still had him on her side.

"So, sometimes unconventional can work for conventional lessons, wouldn't you agree?" she asked.

Mr. Perkins smiled. "You have me there, Miss Wright." He picked up his things from her desk, still swiping at his suit with his free hand. "Well, if you can bring up this school's reading scores using some of these methods, then we'll give your school a second chance. I'm interested to see how all of this fun," he indicated the Pompeii project with a sweep of his hand, "stands up on a test paper."

Then he was gone, taking his notebook and pencil with him.

Nate crossed the room to her, shared triumph in his chocolate gaze. For a second, it felt like old times. Her and Nate against the world.

"We won that battle," Nate said, his voice low in her ear and setting off an eruption of its own. Every time the man was near her, heat coiled between them, awakening the sleeping memories of the times they used to share.

"But not the war," she said, reminding him, and herself, that there were other goals here. She shouldn't think about herself, her heart or the simmering need growing in volume inside her.

"Not yet, Jenny, not yet." His gaze met hers and for a long, long second, she wasn't sure if he was talking about the classroom or them. "But we will. Somehow."

"I don't know what you did, Miss Wright," Dr. Davis said, approaching Jenny as she and Nate were cleaning up the classroom at the end of the day, "but please do it again tomorrow."

Jenny blinked. Had that been a *compliment* from the principal? "I don't think I did anything different today than on any other day."

"You impressed Howard Perkins. He's going to give a glowing report to the board this afternoon after he returns. That's one in our corner. If I could, I'd give you a raise and a company car for that one." Dr. Davis grinned. Actually grinned.

Had Dr. Davis been inhaling from the school's helium tank? She looked happier than Jenny had ever seen her. "I'm very glad to hear that," Jenny said. "I hope this means good things for Mercy Elementary."

"You and I both, Miss Wright." Dr.

Davis gave Nate a nod. "I hear you were also instrumental in making this class great today, Mr. Dole. Mr. Perkins said you were a 'wonderful addition to the classroom environment.' That's a direct quote, by the way."

"Just doing my job," he said.

"Well, I'll see you both in the morning." Then Dr. Davis walked off, humming a jaunty tune under her breath, a light step in her walk that hadn't been there a week ago.

"What was in the school lunch today?" Jenny asked, returning to her desk now that the children were gone and the chairs put up for the night. "I've never seen her this happy."

"Don't knock it. It's a nice change from earlier in the week. The dragon has become a dragonfly, I think."

She grinned. "You are terrible."

"I try."

Jenny paused, the red grading pen in her hand. "I want to thank you for what you did with Mr. Perkins today. You . . ." She drew in a breath instead of finishing the sentence.

"Go ahead. You can say it. I was right."

She pursed her lips. "I hate to admit that, you know."

"Yep. But I love to hear it all the same."

"Okay. I'll say it. You were right. A little help, *once in a while, isn't bad.*" Jenny directed her pen at him. "But I don't need you fighting all my battles. I'm quite capable on my own."

"I noticed that." The tease in his eyes disappeared, replaced by something heated. "You've grown up into a hell of a woman, Jenny Wright."

She inhaled, before she forgot to breathe. "And you've grown up, too. Into more of a man than you ever were."

He grinned. "I wasn't sure you'd noticed."

She swallowed. "I noticed, Nate." Every second of the day. In her dreams at night. In her thoughts, anticipating when he'd arrive in the classroom.

Oh, yeah, she'd noticed.

When they'd broken up, they'd still essentially been kids at twenty years old. Jenny, a couple years into college, Nate partway through his first tour in the marines. They'd barely known what they wanted out of life then. But now, they were adults, and knowing what they wanted wasn't the problem. That, Jenny could see in Nate's eyes, and feel in the answer churning within herself.

Having what they wanted, without it hurting themselves or anything else — *that* was the problem.

"We've had such a great day, I say we go out and celebrate," Nate said.

"Celebrate?" That hadn't been where her thoughts were leading. Not unless his idea of a celebration involved lip locking and Makeout Hill.

"Let's go down to Sam's Sweet Scoop and split a sundae."

He meant ice cream. Not anything else. Jenny dropped her gaze to the work before her. If she were smart, she'd stay here and away from re-involving herself with Nate. They might be grown up now, but that didn't mean he wanted what she did out of life or that any of the problems they'd had nine years ago had disappeared. If anything, the problems had grown up, too. "I shouldn't. I have the math tests to grade and the essays to look over —"

"I'll help you." He grinned. "If you help me polish off a banana split."

She put down her red pen and looked up at him. "You sure know the way to a girl's heart."

"I remember what you used to like. Banana splits were your favorites."

He remembered. What other things did

he remember? The way she liked to be kissed? The way she liked him to hold her? Her memories warred with the saner parts of her that told her going out with Nate only opened up an old wound that had never really healed.

"Only the chocolate and marshmallow parts," Jenny said, focusing her mind on ice cream, not the mind-melting thoughts of Nate. "I left the pineapple end for you."

"I think it's a good trade. Sharing an ice cream with you, in exchange for grading a few tests."

"You don't know what you're getting yourself into," she said, holding up the thirty-question math test as proof.

"Oh, yes, I do, Jenny." But when his gaze met hers, she had to wonder if even *she* knew what she was getting herself into.

Sam's Sweet Scoop was teeming with after-school activity. The advent of spring had everyone out, ready to start indulging in icy treats a little early. Miss Tanner and Miss Marchand sat at one of the outside tables, ice creams of their own before them and one banana split on the ground for Miss Tanner's enormous Doberman, Sweet Pea.

Nate and Jenny made their way into the

small bright shop. Nate held the glass door for her and let her pass through first. She brushed against his chest as she did. The touch of him against her awakened a hundred nerve endings and memories from years ago. Oh, she knew the feel of his chest. Her brain had never forgotten the pattern of those muscles, the feel of the hard ridges.

For just a second, she wanted to step back from her organized, scheduled life, to lean against his chest and let him carry the burden.

She'd done that in the past, and he had let her down by leaving her over and over again, then distancing himself emotionally. So she'd learned to take care of herself, to put everything into straight little organizational lines. Not to depend on a man, especially this man, who jetted off to the next adventure just when she needed him most. She wasn't about to change that now.

"Crowded in here, isn't it?"

So he'd noticed their close quarters, too. "Yes, very." He stood behind her in line, pressed in by the crowd of people anxious for a double-dipped vanilla cone.

"Makes waiting in line more bearable," he said in her ear.

Makes it unbearable, she thought.

Makes it impossible for me to think. To breathe. To remember exactly why I thought getting involved again with Nate was a bad idea.

"Next!" the kid at the counter called, waving them forward, his white envelope-shaped hat bobbing on his head. Jenny moved forward with Nate. "A dish of chocolate please," she said.

"Oh, come on, live a little," Nate said. "Go for the whole shebang."

"I shouldn't. It's bad for —"

"For what? It's one dessert. Not a lifetime of bad habits." Nate turned to the server. "One banana split, extra toppings, nuts and whipped cream."

"You got it." The kid turned away and prepared their order, swirling the whipped cream on top like snow on a mountain.

Jenny's mouth began to water. She looked at her lowly dish of chocolate ice cream beside the banana split masterpiece and hated to admit Nate was right. She hadn't had one of those in so long. Probably since she and Nate had last been here together. "All right, you win," she said. "I'll trade you."

"Oh, no doing." He picked up his boat-shaped bowl and held it close to his chest. "But I'll share. And I'll even feed you a couple of bites."

Heat quickened in her gut at that thought. Oh, that would be wrong. Very wrong. But so much more delicious than just the ice cream itself.

Nate paid the server, tucked his cane under one arm and picked up the second dish, too, turning toward the outdoor tables. "Ladies first."

"Let me get one of those for you."

"Let me be a gentleman and spoil you."

When was the last time a man had spoiled her? Heck, when was the last time she'd been out with a man, never mind let one take the lead? Months, she knew.

"Okay, I will. But only because my last date was so horrible and I think I deserve a little spoiling."

They selected a table by the sidewalk. A bright-red umbrella shaded the round white table, surrounded by a pair of white wicker chairs. Jenny sat and took her bowl of chocolate. Nate pulled his seat close to hers.

"So who was your last date? Dave?"

She laughed. "No, not Dave. I've never gone out with Dave Brooks, no matter how many times he's asked." Was that relief she'd seen in Nate's eyes? Perhaps Nate had been a little jealous of the friendship she'd built up over the years with his old best friend. "My last date was with Gerry Herber, who teaches woodshop at the middle school. He spent the whole night talking about how building a birdhouse teaches teenage boys about life."

Nate chuckled. "That might be a bit of a stretch."

"Oh, he had more theories, like one about how a good hammer can set you on the right path. A bad hammer is bad karma. And choosing the wrong length nail for the job —"

"Will make for twice as much work in the end."

She laughed. "Yeah, something like that."

The spring breezes whispered between them, a hint of a chill still in the air, but not enough that Jenny wanted to go back inside. Birds chirped from nearby trees and people strolled along the sidewalk, clearly enjoying the taste of the next season.

"Are you ready?" Nate asked.

"For what?"

"For your bite of heaven." He held out a spoonful of banana split, chocolate sauce coating the cold vanilla ice cream. It did, indeed, look like heaven on a plastic spoon.

Her gaze went to his eyes. She suspected the bite of heaven wasn't in the dessert at all. Being here with him was a mistake. She was already wrapped up in him again. Thinking about kissing him, touching him . . .

Loving him. All over again.

Instead of doing any of those crazy things, Jenny opened her mouth and took the bite of sundae. As promised, it tasted amazing. "Sam's Sweet Scoop never disappoints," she said after she swallowed.

"Nice to know some things stay the same," Nate said quietly. He reached for her hand, clasping it in his own. "Jenny, I want to ask you —"

"Why if it isn't Miss Wright! Fancy running into you here!"

Jenny didn't need to turn around to know who was behind her. Ed Spangler. The Animals Where You Want 'Em guy. In a public place. With her. Again.

She sent up a quick prayer that he was here without an omnivorous companion and turned around, a smile plastered on her face. "Mr. Spangler. Nice to see you again." *Not.*

"I was here in town, going after Eloise again," Ed explained. "She is one determined heifer when she's got her mind on Larry Bertram's bull." He gestured behind him at the aforementioned Eloise, hitched up in the back of a pickup truck and looking quite unhappy about having to go home without her true love.

"I'll bet she is," Jenny managed. Beside her, she saw Nate smirk.

"I wanted to thank you for how gracious you've been with my animals," Ed said. He removed his hat and clutched it to his overalls. "Not all people like kissing a pig or a goat. But you, you've always been real nice to my animals and real patient with me. I'm afraid my antics might have gotten you in a little trouble with your boss."

"It worked out all right." She hoped. But she wasn't going to tell Ed Spangler that. All she needed was for him to show up in Dr. Davis's office with a baby chick as an apology gift.

"I think what you're doing with those kids is mighty admirable. Getting them to read and everything. And Reginald thinks so, too."

An endorsement from a kissing pig. That should carry her far down the unemployment line. "Thank you."

"Anyway," he added, replacing his hat on his head, "I just wanted to say I'm glad to see a teacher who ain't too fired up about rules and such."

Behind him, Eloise let out a moo.

"Well," Ed said, "I guess that's my cue to go. You have a nice day. And if you ever need another animal, you just call me, Ed Spangler, Animals Where You Want 'Em." He grinned. "I got a llama who's mighty friendly. You'd like her."

Then he was gone, riding off in his bright pink pickup truck at a turtle's pace, Eloise bobbing along in the back.

"A llama? Now that's one I hadn't thought of," Nate said.

"Don't. Dr. Davis will have a heart attack if I bring in one more animal."

"Aw, you're no fun. What happened to the Jenny I used to know? The one who broke all the rules and didn't care?" He moved the banana split in front of her and watched as she dug in, ignoring the uneaten dish of plain chocolate. "Remember the time you and I released those tadpoles into the goldfish tank in Miss Marchand's room?"

"And then had to fish them all out by hand?"

"What about the time we covered all the lockers in the high school with green construction paper for St. Patrick's Day?"

She swallowed the bite of ice cream and nodded. "And had to serve three days of detention."

"And when we went skinny-dipping in the pond behind the Emery Farm?"

The air between them stilled. The thread of tension between them, always there from the minute she'd seen him again, suddenly went taut at the memory.

The heat of a blush filled Jenny's cheeks. She remembered that night. Every second of that night. So many times, when she'd been alone, she'd brought back that memory, one of the ones with Nate that had been her happiest. When they'd been most in love and thought nothing could ever break them apart. "You're just lucky we didn't get caught," she said finally.

Nate shook his head. "What happened to you, Jenny? You used to be . . ."

"Fun? I am fun. Ed Spangler just said so."

"You *are* in your classroom, but it's like you use it all up there. And the rest of your life has no room for fun anymore."

She picked at the banana split, but found her appetite for the dessert had waned. "It's easier this way."

"For what?"

"Just easier, Nate. I'm grown up now. I don't do those kinds of things anymore."

"What, no more skinny-dipping?" He seemed to tease her with his smile, but there was more in his words than he was saying.

She felt a prick of regret for those days, but pushed it away. The last thing Jenny needed in her life right now was a complication. A six-foot-tall marine was the biggest — and strongest — complication she knew.

"No. Not anymore." She offered him more of the ice cream, but he shook his head, so she got to her feet and threw out the remains of their treat.

He joined her and they began to walk toward the park, located just across the street. A few couples strolled along the paved pathways of the park, some mothers pushed their babies in strollers, a few kids ran from tree to tree, playing a game. But overall, most of the activity was across the street, leaving them alone.

"Was I that terrible to you?"

"What do you mean?"

"When we broke up. You've changed so much since then. I hate to think I was the cause of that."

She spun toward him. "You know, Nate, not everything is about you and me. Or a relationship we had nine years ago. Maybe I like order in my life for another reason. It keeps me on track. And maybe it has nothing at all to do with you."

"If it has nothing to do with me, then why won't you take a chance and date me again?"

She strolled along the paved pathway, barely seeing the new buds of grass, the fresh tulips blooming along the edges. The scent of new beginnings hung in the air, but not between her and Nate.

"Maybe I'm not interested in you anymore," she said. "Did you ever think of that? Maybe I'm not attracted to you. Maybe I don't think we have anything in common anymore."

"Really?" He took her hand, stopping her in her tracks, and brought it to his lips, but didn't kiss it, just held it there, her delicate fingers in his large palm, a tease and a tempt all at once. She felt like a hummingbird in his grasp, fragile and delicate, yet protected from the strong winds of life. "So if I turned your hand over," and he did just that as he said the words, "and kissed your palm, then kissed a trail back up to those lips that I have missed for nearly a decade, you wouldn't want one bit of that?"

She swallowed. "No."

He tugged her hand, drawing her closer, pulling her into his space. She felt as if she was on his territory now, as if she had lost her footing. "And if I said I was sorry and I'd been stupid for letting you go, would that make any difference at all?"

"No." But her heart told her she was lying. To herself, to him.

He stared at her, long and hard. She felt the sting of tears in the back of her eyes but she wouldn't let them show. She couldn't get involved with Nate again. She couldn't afford another heartbreak like the one she'd had before.

Jenny knew, deep in her heart, that if she fell for Nate again, this time it would be permanent. No matter how much older she was now, she didn't have the strength to pick up the pieces after Nate left her a second time. And he would.

If there was anything Nate Dole was good at, it was leaving.

"Then fine. I'll leave you alone. We'll stick to classroom business only." He released her hand and stepped away. "Good day, Miss Wright."

Then he turned and left, leaving Jenny alone in the park with plenty to regret and the plaintive, lonely wails of one heart-broken cow in the background.

Chapter Eight

★ ★ ★

Jenny sat in the small, tidy living room of her grandfather's apartment, sipping a cup of tea on Thursday night and told herself men were more aggravation than they were worth. The past two days with Nate in her classroom had been pure torture. He had, as promised, been all business. He'd come in a few minutes before class started, then left as soon as the day was over. When the children were there, he was all smiles and fun, but no more friendly to Jenny than her orthodontist.

She'd come over to her grandfather's house, hoping that seeing him would get her mind off the stubborn marine in her life. If anything, her recalcitrant grandfather served as an even bigger reminder of Nate.

"Grandpa, going for a walk with Spike will not kill you. Or the dog. It will be good for both of you."

"I'm quite happy in my chair." Richard

Wright settled himself further into his recliner, his thumb on the remote. In front of him, Vanna White turned letters with a bright, perfect smile.

"The Mercy Dog Club will be fun. Spike will get to make some friends."

"Jennifer, he's a dog. He doesn't need friends. He has me."

She rose, came around to the front of his chair and put her hands on her hips. "Exactly, Grandpa."

"Are you saying I'm not a good friend for my dog?"

She crossed her arms over her chest. "You think Spike gets a kick out of *Wheel of Fortune*?"

Her grandfather looked down at his Jack Russell terrier, lying against the chair, head on paws, eyes closed. "He can whine the letter *E,* you know. He'd be a great contestant on *Wheel,* if only Pat Sajak would let an animal on once in a while."

"Grandpa!"

"Oh, all right. I'll go. But only if you go with me." His blue eyes twinkled with mischief.

"I am not —"

"You want to make sure I actually go, right? I could change my mind halfway there and turn around. I am an old man, you know. Feeble-minded and forgetful. Could take twenty steps and get myself lost." He barely disguised the grin under his short white beard.

She'd been successfully blackmailed by a man nearly three times her age. "Well then, you're just going to have to wonder all night what Vanna's hiding behind the clue of 'Thing' with the letters T, L, N and E in it because I'm ready to go right now."

Her grandfather rolled his eyes but popped the recliner back into place and got to his feet. Together, they leashed Spike, who looked at his master with a question in his eyes when the leather lead was snapped onto his collar.

A few minutes later, an overjoyed Spike, a complaining Grandpa and Jenny were at the park, where another dozen or so dogs and their masters were milling about while a couple of volunteers set up jumping posts and climbing games.

"Spike's not going to like this," her grandfather said.

"Spike would drag you over to the park every day if he could," she said, gesturing toward the dog. "Look at him. He's in terrier heaven."

Spike was, indeed, leaning toward the group. Her grandfather gave Jenny one more look of protest, but Jenny cut it off with a shake of her head and a gentle push in the direction of the Mercy Dog Club.

"I'm cutting you out of my will for this, Jennifer."

"I've already cut you out of mine for being so cantankerous," she said. Then she grinned at him and joined him on the path that led to the other pet owners.

Along the opposite side of the circle, she saw the Misses. Poor Miss Tanner was trying desperately to corral her determined Doberman, Sweet Pea, and keep him on the path. The big black and brown dog had other ideas — like squirrel chasing — and kept tugging Miss Tanner off the pathway and into the woods. Miss Marchand and the dainty Sugarplum strolled around the circle, navigating the crowd and talking with Miss Tanner on the odd moments when the dog allowed her back into the group.

A hole opened up in the crowd, allowing her to see the people on the other side of the Misses. Jenny blinked, then looked again.

Of all the residents of Mercy that Jenny expected to see walking a dog around the town park, Nate Dole wouldn't even have made the list.

But there he was — and he wasn't alone.

He was accompanied by a medium-sized . . . well, mutt. The dog was a motley mix of terrier and maybe spaniel, its coat a muddle of brown and white shortish, wiry hair. Neither Nate nor the dog moved fast, mainly because of Nate's knee, Jenny figured.

"Isn't that Nate Dole?" her grandfather asked, gesturing across the way.

"Yeah, he's back in town."

"You knew this, and didn't say one word?"

"I didn't think it was important."

Grandpa raised a suspicious brow at her. "Jennifer, I know you too well. The things you don't mention are the ones that are the most important. How long has he been back?"

"I'm not sure. A few days, I guess."

"And have you seen him?"

She let out a sigh. Grandpa would ferret out the truth eventually. Besides, the entire Mercy gossip chain was represented here today and inevitably, someone would start talking about Nate being back and in Jenny's class. "Every day this week. He's helping out in my classroom *only,*" she hastened to add. "A kind of joint project between his mother and Dr. Davis."

"Grace? Why is she involved with something at the school?"

"I think she thought it would do him good to get out of the house, exercise his knee. So, Dr. Davis put him in my classroom."

"Because . . . you asked for him?"

"No. Not at all. It was a fluke. I didn't mention our history."

Her grandfather cast her a sideways glance, then looked to Nate, fifty yards away. "Seems that history still exists. You going to do anything about it?"

"I don't want to get hurt again, Grandpa." Since the death of her father, she'd become close to her grandfather, with him serving as a surrogate parent. Her mother had never been much for long talks, being an impatient woman more given to spontaneous trips out-of-state than heart-to-hearts with her only child.

Her grandfather laid a gentle hand on her arm and met her gaze with one filled with love and years of wisdom. "You can't live your whole life being afraid of getting hurt, honey. The more you try to control things, the more they escape your grasp."

Something an awful lot like tears stung in Jenny's eyes but she blinked and the feeling went away. "We're here to walk Spike, not talk about my love life."

Her grandfather gave her a grin. "I am perfectly capable of walking my own dog. I think, my dear, you should go over and talk to Nate. You need that more than hanging out with an old fuddy-duddy like me." Before she could protest, her grandfather marched off, with Spike in tow, leaving her to either stand there, dog-less like the lone cat in a kennel of puppies, or do exactly what her grandfather had said.

That was the problem with older people. They had the upper hand of experience when it came to manipulation.

Jenny crossed to Nate. Only to satisfy her curiosity, she told herself. And because her grandfather was practically dislocating his shoulder giving her a hinting wave from his side of the circle. "Since when did you get a dog?" she asked.

"This afternoon." He grinned. "I stopped by the Lawford Animal Shelter after school and found Harry there, looking for a home."

"Harry?"

"He looked like a Harry to me."

She laughed. "I suppose he does at that. What on earth made you get a dog?"

He shrugged. "I needed some companionship. I'm used to living with a platoon of guys. Being in that house by myself is a bit lonely, you know. Plus, I needed a way to exercise my knee. Treadmills bore the hell out of me, so I thought this would be more fun."

He started to walk around the circular track marked out on the grass with some rope by the volunteers. Harry hobbled along beside him on the opposite side of his cane.

"Is there something wrong with him? He seems to be having trouble walking."

"He was hit by a car a while back. Dr. McAllister said he was hurt pretty bad and his leg never really healed the same. He's got a limp."

"Like you," she said softly.

"Yeah, like me."

Nate had adopted the one dog no one would have wanted. Because he'd been lonely. The shock of that hit Jenny in the stomach. In all the years she'd known Nate, he'd never, ever expressed any kind of inner weakness like that. Now here he was, letting her see inside and telling her he'd felt doubt, loneliness, worry.

He had opened up and let her see inside him. That was not the Nate she expected.

Had he changed?

"A dog is a kind of permanent thing, you know," she said.

"I know."

He didn't elaborate. Curiosity burned on the tip of her tongue. If he had a dog, he couldn't be going back to the marines. It certainly wasn't something he could take on missions or leave at the base to be baby-sat by a bunch of grunts. She knew Grace Dole already had a couple of spaniels and doubted his mother would want another dog underfoot in her busy household. Finally, she asked the question anyway. "But . . . what are you going to do with him when you have to go back to the marines?"

Nate's gaze traveled across the field, lingering on some distant spot in the woods. Behind them, dogs yipped greetings to each other and owners traded pet pride stories.

"I'm not going back." His voice was low and quiet, almost inaudible in the busy park.

"You're not? But . . . but . . . the marines is everything to you. That's who you are — Nate Dole, the marine."

He took a long breath, then stopped walking and turned to face her. "Would it make a difference to you if I wasn't a marine anymore?"

She blinked. "Of course not."

Nate heard the conviction in her voice and knew Jenny was telling the truth. Had he been worrying himself over nothing all this time? Had he not known Jenny the way he thought? Or had he been too caught up in his superhero image to remember that she had known him before he was a marine? That she knew the Nate he'd always been.

And maybe she didn't need him to be a marine to be a part of her life.

The thought stunned him, rocked all the convictions he'd been holding onto so tightly and shoved them overboard into new waters. Nate took in another breath and looked into her deep emerald eyes. "Then let's get out of here. I need to tell you something."

They went to Nate's little ranch house, which was only a couple of blocks away from the park. Clouds had moved in, blocking the sun, and adding a chill to the late March air, so they opted to go inside instead of sitting on the porch swing. Nate lit a fire in his fireplace and put on the coffeepot. Stall tactics, he knew, but he needed a few minutes to find the words he wanted to say.

Jenny waited patiently on the sofa, Harry lying by her feet and gnawing on a rawhide bone. She'd offered to help, but Nate had refused. For some reason, he needed to do these silly little tasks on his own, if only to prove to her that he wasn't completely handicapped.

He came back into the living room, two mugs in one hand, the stupid, ridiculous cane in the other. He handed her a cup, then took a seat across from her in a wingback chair he'd inherited from his mother. If it wasn't for his mother, he wouldn't have any furniture at all. That was top on his list. Get himself some real furniture. Something that looked like him, not a mishmash from his mother's house. As much as he loved his mother, he didn't share her love of chintz.

He was glad he'd taken the time that morning to pick up a little, toss the old newspapers into the recycle bin and get his laundry into a basket. He looked less like a slob and more like someone who could have a little company.

Some particular company named Jenny. Maybe, if he could make things right between them, that company would be here every night and every day.

"When I was in Afghanistan in January,"

he began, setting his mug on an end table and ignoring the coffee for now, "our base was involved in a firefight. We didn't sustain a lot of casualties, but I got hit."

She looked at his knee. "In your leg." It wasn't a question.

He nodded. "The bullet did a lot of damage. Too much. My knee is permanently messed up. Doc said I'll always walk with a limp."

"But . . ." She looked at him and put the pieces together. "That's why you quit, isn't it?"

He rose and crossed to the fireplace, bending to stir at the fire with a poker. The embers flared when he did, flames licking at the kindling. "When I realized I couldn't be any good to the team anymore . . . I knew it was time to go."

"Nate, I'm sure there are other things you can do in the marines."

He rose and turned toward her, the heat at his back. "Not me, Jenny. I was too used to being the rescuer, the guy you called in when things went wrong. I couldn't sit by and watch all the action and not go crazy."

"What are you going to do now?"

He shrugged. "Until you came along and got me off the couch, I was having a damned fine pity party."

"You? You were always the strong one."

His gaze went to the window. Outside, Mercy went on as it always had. A neighbor watered his lawn, an elderly woman played catch with her grandson on a pristine front lawn. A loose beagle sniffed at the trash cans put out for tomorrow's pickup. Life as he'd known it, from inside this house. "Even superheroes have a weak spot, Jenny."

Then she rose and did what he hadn't expected. She crossed to him, took his hands with her own and drew him back down to the sofa with her, one step at a time, accepting him as he was and bringing him into the circle of Jenny. There was no rejection in her eyes, no disapproval. Only the same steady emerald gaze he'd known most of his life. Something warm and content settled in his chest.

"I never knew," she said.

"No one knows. You're the first person I told."

"You haven't even told your family?"

"I've done a good job of avoiding them since I got home." He let out a breath. "I'm a marine, Jenny. That's who I am. Now, to say I'm not one anymore, it's just . . ." He looked away for a second, collecting his thoughts, then returned to her gaze. "It's like I'm not me anymore."

Jenny smiled and reached up, cupping Nate's face with her hands. "You were always Nate. Not Nate the marine."

"I think I'm just starting to realize that, after this week."

Her touch on his face was soothing, yet at the same time ignited something within him that he'd tried to tamp down for days, because she'd asked him to, making it clear she didn't want to get involved with him again. But if that were so, then why was she here, her eyes looking into his, filled with concern . . . and maybe something more?

When he caught Jenny's gaze, Nate dared to do something he hadn't done in what felt like a hundred years. Hope.

He leaned toward Jenny, his palm over hers on his face, pulling her hand into his. "I've missed you, Jenny. More than you can ever know."

She began to protest. To hell with it all.

He cut her off with the best way he knew how. By kissing her. She could slap him, damn it, and it would be a well-deserved hit, but if he didn't kiss her now, and answer once and for all whether or not she still cared about him, he'd go crazy.

Because he sure as hell still cared about her.

She didn't slap him. She didn't pull away. Jenny only hesitated for a split second and then seemed to melt into him, as if his movement had broken down some wall between them.

She tasted of honey and cinnamon, like cookies he'd been forbidden to eat and then handed on a delicate china platter. He inhaled the scent of her hair, the warm, fresh sandalwood scent of her skin. He wished he could bottle everything about Jenny and keep it with him for the days when they would inevitably be apart again.

Her mouth opened against his, a tiny moan escaping her lips and as if in concert, they moved closer, arms embracing, torsos meeting.

It had been nine years since he'd kissed Jenny but it felt like yesterday and a century ago all at the same time. Fireworks exploded within his head. He wanted more, he wanted everything. He wanted her.

His hands tangled in her hair, in that gold silk, remembering all over again how wonderful it was to hold Jenny. Everything about her felt the same, as if no time at all had passed since the last time they'd been together. She fitted against him perfectly, sliding into the space against his chest with ease.

"Oh, Nate, I've missed you, too." Her words whispered out on a breath. She kissed his lips, his cheeks, the bridge of his nose. "All of you."

He echoed her kisses, tasting her cheeks, her lips, the side of her neck. Nibbling along the one place in the curve of her throat where he knew she loved to be kissed.

She let out a gasp and pressed harder against him. His hand slipped up between them, against the soft cotton fabric of her shirt, cupping her breast. She felt like the sweetest memory he'd ever had, the incarnation of all those dreams that had gotten him through so many lonely nights and horribly long days in sweaty jungles and barren deserts.

"Jenny, I —" His words were cut off by the introduction of a wet, determined nose against his arm.

Harry.

Harry, needing something a little more urgent than Nate did right now. Or at least Harry seemed to think it was more urgent.

Nate, however, would beg to differ.

Chapter Nine

★ ★ ★

A few minutes later, Jenny was back in Nate's arms and Harry was back with his rawhide. Nate had herded the poor dog in and out of the house in a flash, probably giving Harry a heart attack in the process of his lawn visit.

"I have a horrible idea," Nate said now. A devilish twinkle lit his brown eyes.

She laughed. "Then I probably don't want to hear it."

He clasped her hands with his. "Let's take Miss Marchand's advice. Revisit a few old haunts. Resurrect a few old memories."

"Which old memories? Specifically?" She narrowed her gaze.

He grinned. "The skinny-dipping one. To be exact."

"Nate! It's the end of March. I know the first day of spring has come and gone, but it's still only about forty degrees out at night. And the water temperature —" She shuddered.

167

"Not in a lake, silly. Even I'm not that adventurous." He lowered his mouth to her neck and whispered the words against the hollow of her throat. "In a hot tub."

She gasped. "You have got to be kidding me. Where would we find one? I don't own one. You don't own one and I'm not getting completely naked with you. Besides, neither one of us has on swimsuits." She pulled back and wagged a finger at him. "And just because we're discussing this doesn't mean I'm considering this crazy idea of yours."

"Jenny, Jenny, Jenny, those are mere speed bumps in our plan." His grin widened.

"I thought you told Dave you gave up your partying ways."

"I did. Except when it comes to you."

When he said those words, deep and husky, something within her stirred. The part of her she thought she'd turned off after they'd broken up, the part she'd tried to tamp down with schedules and organization charts and filing cabinets. When they'd dated, life with Nate had been crazy, spontaneous and . . .

Fun. More fun than anything she could remember. Not the kind of unpredictability of her childhood, but a sort of combined impulsiveness that only the two of them could create together.

With him looking at her like that and his voice in that deep range only Nate seemed to possess, as if he had a radio band linked straight to her heart, she wanted those days back again. Just for tonight.

One time. What could it hurt? A little fun. Then she could go back to living her life by her watch and her calendar.

"Where do you propose we find a hot tub?" she asked. "And what do we do about the swimsuit problem?"

Nate's smile stretched from ear to ear and the heat in his gaze sizzled hotter than an August day. "We'll improvise."

And with that, Jenny knew she was in for a lot of fun — and a lot more than she'd bargained for.

"What happens if we get caught?" Jenny asked twenty minutes later. She stood on the concrete slab ringing Luke and Anita's hot tub, her shoes in her hands and her second thoughts doing somersaults in her stomach.

"Since when did you ever worry about that?"

"Since I became a third-grade teacher in this town. I can get caught on the front page of the *News* kissing a pig, but stealing some hot-tub time would not make for good publicity for my career."

"It's my brother's house, so I doubt he'd call in the local reporters. Plus, he and Anita aren't home. I already checked. Probably attending something tonight at Emily's school. The water is hot and all it needs now is you and me."

"It's cold outside."

He directed a thumb in the direction of the bubbling jets. "But it's warm in there."

"This is insane."

"Yes. It is. I agree with you. We haven't done anything this crazy since we were teenagers." He stepped closer to her, clutching her jacket in his hands and peeling it out of her grasp. "Which is all the more reason why we should do it now."

"I . . ." She looked at the tub, her sentence trailing off.

"I promise to be a good boy in there. Most of the time." He smirked.

"We still didn't solve the swimsuit issue."

"Hmm. We didn't, did we?" He pushed her jacket off her shoulders and to the ground. With it, her shoes tumbled out of her hands, landing with double clonks on the concrete. "You're wearing a sweater.

That won't work in a hot tub."

"No, it won't." The words came out soft and breathless.

"Khaki pants won't cut it either."

"No, uh . . . they won't." She must have left her brain cells back in the car because looking at him right now, she couldn't form a single coherent thought.

His mouth turned up on one corner. "Then I guess you'll just have to go in your skivvies."

"That's playing with fire."

"I'm a big boy. I can handle it." He tossed his jacket onto a patio chair beside them, then took off his cream-colored polo shirt and added it to the pile. "What I really worry about is whether *you* can control *yourself*."

"No worries here." At least her words sounded sure.

"Really?" He undid his belt buckle, then slipped his dark-blue trousers to the ground and kicked them, along with his shoes, over to the chair. He stood before her in a pair of cranberry silk boxers and nothing else.

Need surged within Jenny. She wanted to touch his skin, to put her hand on either side of the hard planes of his chest, to press herself to his skin and taste what she had lost so many years ago.

The memory of them skinny-dipping in the lake a decade ago came rocketing back. The tease of the water on their skin, the seductive play of the waves, the slippery movement of skin against skin. And then finally, them sharing themselves with each other, ending the long months of waiting, sealing a love they'd thought would last forever.

She'd missed that feeling. She'd missed him. And God help her, but she wanted to feel all of it again, if only for tonight. His skin was prickling in the cold, but he waited, silent, knowing she was making up her mind.

There really wasn't a decision to be made. Her mind had been made up the minute she'd set foot on his porch last Sunday and he'd opened the door to her, surprise and joy in his eyes.

Her hands went to her sweater and she lifted it up and over her head, tossing it onto the chair. His eyes widened, as they had that first day they'd met again, with the same mixture of surprise and delight.

He watched as Jenny slid off her pants and threw them to the side. She stood there, in only a simple lace-trimmed white bra and panties, a surge of desire running through her when his eyes darkened with an answering need. Then the cold air hit her legs and torso like a slap across the face. "Okay, whose idea was this again?"

"It's a lot better to hot tub *in* the hot tub than stand outside it and freeze to death," Nate said. He put out his hand. "Come on."

She took his hand and followed him up the steps, the full meaning of what they were doing quickening in her veins. This was wrong. But not so wrong they could be sent to jail. It was only . . . a little illicit. And for a woman who hadn't broken a rule in nearly a decade, that was enough to get her blood rolling.

Maybe it was just the company. She looked at Nate as he eased himself into the water, his face the picture of bliss. She wanted a little of that, too.

In an instant, she was in the water beside him. Warmth seeped into her skin, covering her up to her neck. Nate scooted beside her, wrapping his arm around her bare waist.

A searing flame shot through Jenny at his touch. The fabric of their underclothes seemed to disappear in the water; there seemed to be nothing between them.

"Comfortable?" he asked. His voice

sounded low and heavy, as if he'd weighted it with gravel.

"Yes . . . No. Oh, Nate, this is . . ."

"Hot?"

"Yeah." Too hot. Too much to handle.

"A bad idea?" he said, as if he'd been reading her mind.

Hearing him actually voice her thoughts made her reconsider her objections. Only because she was so warm and comfortable, of course.

"Well, we are two consenting adults."

"And we're consenting to . . . ?"

"Hot tub," she said. "Nothing more, right?"

He nodded, his arm still around her waist, the heat there hotter than anything she'd felt in a long, long time. "Nothing more than a little spontaneity."

Oh, this was more than spontaneity. This was a prelude to sex, plain and simple. What had she been thinking? Playing with fire only left her burned in the end. And yet, she wanted Nate. She wanted this.

The water bubbled around her, Nate's touch on her waist easy and secure. Everything seemed to wrap her in comfort and sensuality. How long had it been since she'd let down her defenses to just . . . be?

The answer didn't require more than an

instant of thought. A long, long time.

"Do you want to get out?" he asked.

"No. I want —" she began, turning toward him, and then she didn't care anymore what the consequences were or what she was doing. Jenny moved, the water sloshing over the sides of the tub, to sit in front of Nate. She straddled him and pressed her chest to his, every inch of his torso mapped beneath the soaking fabric of her bra. She wrapped her arms around him and then kissed him with all the emotions and the feelings she'd kept pent-up for so many years.

He groaned and opened his mouth to hers, inviting her in. Her hands roamed his back, the water lubricating the journey, sending her fingertips into a sensory overload. Their tongues entwined, memory igniting with new passion.

The alternate feel of the hot below and the cold above only served to intensify everything. Passion for him ignited inside her, an electrical surge demanding more. Demanding it immediately. A nine-year wait to have Nate again had become too damned long. "I want you, Nate," she said. "I want you again. Now. Here."

"Jenny," he growled, her name barely a word coming off his tongue. His hands

slipped between them to cup her breasts, thumbs rolling over the nipples, and she arched backward, sensation surging through her like twin lightning bolts.

"Nate, I — I —"

When he drew his hands up to cup her face, disappointment rocketed through her veins at the loss of his touch on other parts of her. His hands had served a much better purpose . . . elsewhere.

Nate's gaze locked on her eyes. "Oh, Jenny, you have no idea how much I want you now, too. In a blink, I'd make love to you, but —" He paused, and then a smile, the gentlest one she'd ever seen on his face before, crossed his lips. "But I want to do it right this time. Do *everything* right with you this time. And that means no rushing. No acting without thinking first."

Need still pounded in her veins, but she managed to work a mirroring smile onto her face. "We did jump into the hot tub on the spur of the moment."

He grinned. "That we did. But, ah, for something more serious, I want to take it slow." His thumb traced over her lips and Jenny thought there had never been anything sweeter than that simple touch. "Because when — and I mean *when* — we do make love, I want it to last forever."

She blinked and drew back. Had he said what she thought? "Are you talking forever as in some kind of long-weekend thing or . . . the other kind of forever?"

"In my book, Jenny, there's only one kind of forever." Even in the moonlight, she could see which kind he meant in his dark-brown gaze.

Panic rose in her and she opened her mouth to tell him no, that this was too fast, too much, that she didn't have it in her to do this again. Before she could, a pair of headlights illuminated the yard and a voice cut through their hot-tub rendezvous.

"Hey, Dad, there's someone in our hot tub!"

Nate let out a curse. "I think we've been caught."

"Our clothes are on the ground. Our underwear is soaking wet." Despite everything, a giggle escaped Jenny at the absurdity of the situation. "How do you propose we get out of this?"

"Same way we got in. Improvise."

Nate knew he was in trouble when he saw the twinkle in Luke's eye. "Skinny-dipping in my hot tub, little brother?"

"We weren't *completely* naked." He had, more or less, been playing by Jenny's rules.

Luke waved his hand in dismissal. "That's a technicality and you know it. If you were with Jenny, then you're forgiven. Any other woman, and I'll be stringing you up on the front porch."

Nate laughed. "Yeah, it was Jenny. And she's dripping wet and freezing in my car right now, waiting for me to make sure everything's kosher between us."

"It is, except for one thing."

"What?"

Luke gestured at the still steaming hot tub. "You come to Sunday dinner with the family and we'll forget this whole thing happened. Otherwise, I'll have to tell Mom."

"That's the kind of thing you threaten a kid with."

Luke gestured to the still steaming hot tub. "And *that's* the kind of antic a teenager does. A grown man knows better." Luke winked. "Though Anita and I have been known to act like kids ourselves once in a while."

"You're blackmailing me," Nate said.

"Exactly." Luke grinned. "You know you can't hide from your family forever."

"All right. You win. I'll be there for dinner."

"And bring a date. You know how Mom

hates an unbalanced table."

"Have I told you lately that you're a horrible brother?"

"Hey, wait till Mark and Claire get here this weekend from California. Then you'll really be in trouble." Luke gave Nate a clap on the shoulder, then walked back toward his house, laughing.

Anticipation filled Nate's chest as he made his way to his car. Dinner with his family. How long had it been? Too many years, he knew, since he'd had a leave long enough to be home with everyone. With a pang, he realized he'd been crazy to stay away this long, to distance himself over the years.

From them. And from Jenny.

Now all he had to do was convince her to sit across the table from his brother, after just being caught nearly *au naturel* in his backyard. Nate suspected he'd have an easier time getting her entire third-grade class to elect brussels sprouts as the new state vegetable.

"I don't know about this," Jenny said Friday morning. "It sounded like a good idea on Wednesday but now, I'm thinking it's just too crazy."

"What can go wrong? Look at those innocent little faces. Those sweet, trusting eyes. Those teeny-tiny feet. Surely you can't expect anything dreadful to come from such a package?" Nate said.

"Anything that comes in a cage with twenty-four brothers and sisters and is a member of the rodent family spells trouble," Jenny said, giving the cage of white mice a dubious look. "No matter what kind of science lesson they can impart."

Nate had proposed the idea earlier in the week and even set up the arrangement to borrow twenty-five mice from the Lawford Research Facility. She'd thought having live animal behavior experiments would be great at the time, but now, with the mice here, it sounded like the exact kind of insanity Dr. Davis would send her to the firing squad for.

"Oh, cool!" Lindsay exclaimed, running into the classroom, depositing a trail of belongings behind her in her rush. "Mice!"

"They're for the class to study today. And they're not coming out of the cage," Jenny explained. She put her hand over the latch.

"Can't I hold just one?" Lindsay pouted and looked up into Jenny's face, her eyes wide with begging. "Please?"

"No. We're going to watch them navigate mazes, that's all. Then they go back to the research facility."

"Aw, Miss Wright, but he's so cute. I just want to pet his nose. Can I do that, please? Through the cage? With my pinky?"

Jenny didn't bother to point out that the true "him or her" test for a mouse was a little more complicated than a quick exterior visual. Lindsay clasped her hands together and offered up additional pleading.

"All right. Through the cage. One time. And then you have to pick up your things and start your morning work."

Lindsay's one pat turned into a twenty-second affection fest with the plump rodent. She exclaimed over every miniature part of him and tried out all five digits of one hand before deciding her index finger was the best for rubbing him under the chin.

By the time Jenny had shooed Lindsay back to her seat, the other children were in the classroom, crowding around the cage of mice. Nate provided crowd control while Jenny ushered them through in groups of three to see the animals before sending the children off to do their work.

"There, that wasn't so bad," she said once all the children were seated and busy with worksheets.

"I told you. An animal in the classroom doesn't have to be a disaster."

"I think I need to reclassify that statement. A farm animal in the classroom provides a disaster. These ones are quite cute . . . and a nice incentive for getting work done." As they had on the day Nate arrived, the children rushed through their paper, hands shooting up like rockets to announce when they were done.

"Let's get the mice out of the way first, then you can take them back to Lawford Research Facility," Jenny said. "I don't want to take any chances on keeping them in the classroom too long."

"Sounds good." Nate hoisted the maze the lab had sent over onto a long table at the front of the room and connected it to a door on the side of the cage. "All set."

She liked this, she decided, her and Nate working together. They'd made a good team. He'd been able to anticipate her needs and had often stepped in throughout the week with a calming word or a bit of wisdom when the students had a playground dispute. If she hadn't known better, she would have thought Nate was a negotiator, not a master sergeant.

Today, though, their week was over. She

should be glad. The temptation of Nate would be gone in a few hours. Instead, she wished the day wouldn't end, that Fridays had a whole week instead of one short day. He hadn't said what was going to happen tomorrow or Monday, or what he was going to do once he was through with rehab for his knee.

Would he leave? Move on to another city, another place?

Another woman?

The thought speared through her. After the hot-tub incident, she'd made it clear again to Nate that she didn't want a future with him. That she wasn't interested in dating him.

And yet she'd kissed him good-night when he'd dropped her off at home and proven she was a heck of a bad liar. If she could tell him these things from long distance, without the mesmerizing power of his eyes and his touch, then she *might* be able to stick to her resolve.

Now, she realized — too late — that she did indeed want him back. The thought of another woman in his arms . . .

Made her want to curl up and die of heartbreak.

"Jenny? Did you hear me? I said we're all set. And I think the kids are done. Everyone's waiting for you."

"Oh, yeah. Sorry. I was just . . ."

"Daydreaming?" He grinned.

"Yeah."

"If it was about me, then I'll forgive you." A tease lingered in his eyes.

She cocked her head and considered her reply. She could say no, and make up some flimsy lie about work or something stupid like that. Or she could invite chaos right into her life again and tell the truth.

Before he was gone again and she was left with a lot of regrets and nothing else, she turned and smiled at him. "As a matter of fact, I *was* daydreaming about you. And what the future for us might hold."

Then, with a smug and secret smile on her face, Jenny pivoted away from Nate's shocked face and let the first mouse into the maze.

Jimmy, Lindsay, Cole, Alex and Lincoln, so dubbed after their human "sponsors," raced through the maze. Lindsay came out the clear winner — by a nose and a whisker.

"I want a recount!" Jimmy — the student — shouted.

Jenny laughed. "There are no recounts in mouse races."

"Well, I think my mouse should race again. He was checked by Alex's mouse coming around the third corner."

"Okay, okay. We'll let him go once more with the next four."

"Awesome!" Jimmy leaped to his feet, inserting himself right beside the starting point for the race. "Can I raise the door?"

"No, Jimmy, you can't."

"Please? I'll be really careful, I promise."

"All right, but you have to wait until we close the second door and get the other mice inside or we'll have mouse city in the classroom."

"Okay, I will."

Jenny and Nate reached inside the maze, pulling out the five squirming competitors who'd finished the race, then brought over four of them to the opposite cage door to return them to their wood shavings nest.

Jenny raised the door, holding Jimmy's mouse securely in her opposite hand. Nate reached inside for the mice waiting their turn to navigate the maze and selected four, herding them toward the tunnel entrance with a wave of his hand.

"What do we have here?"

Jenny pivoted toward the voice. Howard Perkins, Dr. Davis and someone Jenny didn't recognize stood in the entrance of her room. "Dr. Davis. Mr. Perkins. You're just in time to see our science lesson."

Dr. Davis paled three shades. "Science lesson? With *live* mice?"

Jenny gave a bright, work-with-me-on-this-one nod. "We're studying animal behavior this week."

"And seeing who's got the fastest mouse this side of the Mississ . . . Missi . . . uh, river," Lionel piped up.

"Miss Wright, you always have something fun for me to look forward to," Mr. Perkins said. "If there's anything I enjoy as much as geological studies, it's the study of mammals." He gestured to the man standing beside him. "This is Craig Scott, another member of the accreditation board. I told him what fun we had with your volcano experiment and he came along to judge things for himself. We thought we might bring some of your inventive teaching methods back to the other schools we work with."

"Let's show him now," Jimmy said, jumping forward and raising the starting gate. At the same time, Lionel shoved his way closer, vying to see the start of the race, and knocked the maze off-center from the cage door, leaving an opening, not a tunnel.

"Wait, don't!" Jenny cried. But it was too late.

Dr. Davis, Howard Perkins and Craig Scott were already on their way into the room — at the same time rodent pandemonium was letting loose in grade 3-B.

Dr. Davis's shriek could be heard in a three-county contiguous area. The sound startled the mice even more, sending the flood of white fur scurrying for shelter with all the speed of a tornado warning.

They scampered off the table, down the legs, across the seats, then dispersed when they hit the floor, streaming in every direction at once.

The children laughed — until they saw the mice headed for their feet. Then they were screaming and leaping onto chairs and desks, calling for Jenny to rescue them from the rodent invasion.

"Sit down, please," Jenny yelled above the fracas. No one heard her. Or no one chose to hear her. The children went on panicking, Dr. Davis had slipped into a catatonic state and Howard Perkins was watching with bemused interest.

"Do you have something to catch them with?" Nate asked. "A net? A bowl? Anything?"

Jenny tried to think but nothing came to mind, not with the noise and the panic level rising every second. She turned and grabbed the first thing she saw — a dustpan.

Nate quirked a brow at her, but took the dustpan and set off on a mouse hunt. Jenny dumped out the mini bucket holding her pencils and scissors onto her desk and set off in the opposite direction.

Dr. Davis stared straight ahead, mouth slack. Craig Scott frowned, withdrew a pen from his breast pocket and clicked the point forward.

"This is fascinating," Howard Perkins said to the principal. "Look how they scattered, rather than flocking together. There's safety in numbers but the mice are so confused, they . . ."

Jenny didn't bother listening. She was after the two she'd seen in the corner by Mr. Body's re-assembled torso. She bent down, slid the purple container across the floor and caught half of the pair. One down. Twenty-four to go.

She covered the top with her hand, ran to the cage, got the mouse back inside, then shut and latched the door. The children had stopped screaming and were now giggling, but still perched out of rodent range.

Dr. Davis recovered her composure and directed an evil eye at Jenny. "Miss Wright, you must do something about these animals. Now."

Jenny blew a stray hair out of her face. "I'm trying."

"Aren't they incredible creatures?" Howard Perkins said. "What a great science lesson."

"I think it's a monumental mistake," Craig Scott said. He now had a notepad out and had already filled a page with notations about the event. "This is exactly what we *don't* want in our classrooms."

"It was an accident," Jenny said, then hurried off to catch more.

"Three more down," Nate said, coming up to her with an empty dustpan. "I just made a deposit in the mouse bank."

"This is no time to make jokes." It was chaos. Pure chaos. The exact thing Jenny had avoided all her life, and now here it was, personified in twenty-five mice, in her classroom.

"Don't worry. We'll catch them all."

"Look at their faces," she said, gesturing toward Dr. Davis and the two men by her side, "and then tell me I shouldn't worry."

"We'll get through this, Jenny. You've got a marine on your side." He grinned.

"That's enough ammunition for this battle."

Despite everything, Jenny laughed. She could only pray Nate was right. She readied her bucket, then motioned to him. "Then get to it, soldier, and corral those AWOL rodents. That's an order."

"Yes, ma'am." He gave her a mock salute, then set off, dustpan in hand.

Jenny turned toward her class. The children, clearly less afraid and more intrigued now, were starting to clamber down and look for mice themselves. In the corner, Craig Scott continued to make notes, even going so far as to peek inside the cage and tally the recaptured mice.

"Children, please sit down on your desks," Jenny said. "We'll be able to catch the mice much more easily if everyone stays calm and in one place."

"What if one bites me?" Lindsay asked.

"They won't bite you. Trust me, they're more afraid of you than you are of them."

Lindsay gave Jenny a dubious look and drew her legs up on top of her desk.

"Miss Wright, I cannot recommend that this school retain its accreditation if these are the kinds of 'learning' experiences you have at Mercy Elementary," Craig Scott said, moving toward her, his pen and notepad ready to add any other infractions. "The volcanic explosion Mr. Perkins told me about might have sounded good at first, but I have rethought it now. And this — this is a deplorable situation."

Jenny decided she'd had enough of this. Enough of trying to live up to an impossible standard when she knew her students were doing well and learning. She was trying her hardest, damn it, and what she needed right now was support, not criticism. "Instead of giving me a lecture about the problem, Mr. Scott, you could be part of the solution." She thrust the purple container into his hands. "Please."

Craig Scott blinked at her. He opened his mouth, shut it again, then pivoted and stalked out of the room, with Dr. Davis and Howard Perkins right behind him, leaving Jenny's mouse catcher and her ruined career behind.

"Go after him," Nate said. "I'll keep your class under control."

Debbie had opened the connecting door and poked her head in. "What's going on in here? I heard a bunch of screaming."

"I'd shut that if I were you," Nate told her. "There are mice on the loose here."

Before she could spell *Mickey,* Debbie

had the connecting door slammed shut and locked.

"Are you sure?" Jenny asked him. "There are a lot of mice to catch and the children —"

"We'll be fine. Go save your job. I'll save the classroom from the mice."

Without thinking twice, she rose on her tiptoes and pressed a quick kiss to Nate's cheek. The students noticed the impromptu gesture and let out a few "whoohoos" of appreciation.

Then Jenny spun on her heel, leaving Nate looking as stunned as she felt. She'd only shown him a little gratitude, but given the way her stomach flip-flopped, Jenny realized that had been more than a simple peck on the cheek.

She'd deal with the consequences of *that* later. For now, she had a school and a job to worry about.

In the parking lot, she found Craig Scott, Howard Perkins and Dr. Davis standing in a circle. Dr. Davis's face was pale and drawn, as if she'd aged ten years in the last five minutes.

"I cannot, in good conscience, let a school like this retain its accreditation," Craig Scott was saying. "I'll be speaking to the board immediately about taking action against Mercy Elementary."

"You can't do that," Jenny said, joining the group. "It was just mice."

"Just mice?" He opened his notebook and skimmed a finger along the report inside. "Don't forget, this school also has a history of reading scores and state academic test scores that have dropped each year."

"They won't drop this year," Jenny said. "We're working very hard to encourage reading in our students."

"Too late, Miss Wright." He shut his notebook and headed toward his car. Mr. Perkins stood silent, as if he hadn't decided which side of the fence to sit on yet.

"I won't let you do this," Dr. Davis said. "You will *not* revoke this school's accreditation simply because of one mishap in a third-grade classroom."

Craig Scott pivoted back toward her. "I can. And I will."

"Miss Wright is an excellent teacher. Her class is reading better and more than any third-grade class in the history of this school. *She* is the reason Mercy Elementary is coming around. With her help, we will — and we are — getting back on track."

Craig Scott's lips thinned. He considered Jenny, then Dr. Davis. "Perhaps the problem isn't Miss Wright, but rather you, Dr. Davis?"

Shock washed over the principal's features, then receded. "Maybe it is, Mr. Scott. Maybe I haven't trusted my staff as much as I should have to use their incredible talents to encourage our youngsters to learn." She directed her look at Jenny.

It was an apology, an olive branch for all the years when Dr. Davis had put roadblocks in Jenny's way whenever she'd proposed something new or innovative. Jenny knew she'd be a fool to ignore the gesture. "Dr. Davis is a wonderful principal. We've had some hard years here at Mercy, but we are working together now and we *will* make a difference, Mr. Scott. I assure you. But we can't do that if you won't give us a chance."

He pursed his lips. "Those mice distracted your class today."

"Yes, they did," Jenny said. "They also made the kids laugh and gave them something to talk about for the next three months. And you can bet I won't let this opportunity go by. They'll be writing a short story about a mouse, fictionalizing what just happened. We may have fun, but we'll make it work, too." She gestured toward Mr. Perkins. "That's what we did when the volcano erupted in the classroom, isn't it, Mr. Perkins?"

"The volcano *really* erupted?" Dr. Davis sputtered. To her credit, she bit back her criticism and instead put a tight smile on her face. "How . . . adventurous."

Mr. Perkins nodded, pushing up his glasses as he did. "I had a regular Mount Vesuvius in there. Took out the toothpick city and my suit. But boy, did those kids write some great essays about the experience. I've never seen such work from third-graders. I was impressed."

Craig Scott tapped his toe against the dark black tar of the school parking lot, considering. "You'll have state tests again at the end of the year. If the scores are up —"

"They will be," Jenny and Dr. Davis said at the same time.

"*If* the scores are up, we will allow Mercy Elementary to retain its accreditation." With that, he turned and left.

"You'll do fine," Mr. Perkins said, stepping up to them before joining his fellow board member. "I hear there's a whole section of questions on volcanic activity." He winked, then went on his own way.

After the men were gone, Dr. Davis let

out a long breath. "We're not out of the woods yet."

"No, we aren't. But we have a clear way out of the forest." Jenny smiled and turned toward her boss, who had now become her ally, more or less. "And if we lose our way, we'll just call on Ed Spangler. I'm sure he has an animal for any situation."

Dr. Davis's jaw dropped open. She managed to clamp it, and any protests she might have had, shut. Together, the two of them walked back inside the building. Not really friends, but no longer enemies either.

Cost of one kissing pig — a little bad publicity and the reentry of Nate into her life. Total price undetermined thus far.

Cost of the look on Dr. Davis's face after Jenny mentioned a rerun of Animals Where You Want 'Em — priceless.

Chapter Ten

★ ★ ★

Nate had it all under control by the time Jenny returned to the classroom a few minutes later. She entered the room and paused, brows knitted together when she saw the coordinated, well-behaved activity in her classroom. The students, in groups of five, were canvassing the room, empty paper and tissue boxes in hand. "What are you doing?"

"I separated the students into squads. Each one is responsible for finding mice in a different sector of the room."

She laughed. "Only you would turn a mouse hunt into a war plan."

"We managed to corral all of them except for two." He waved toward the cage where the twenty-three others climbed over each other, safe and secure again.

She nodded, clearly impressed with his work. "Let's hope the remaining two aren't a male and a female."

He grinned. "Yeah, that would create a

whole other slew of problems."

"Thank you," she said. "I really appreciate your help and your mouse-capturing abilities. We'll catch those other two ourselves later. For all we know, they might be on their way to Disney World by now." She grinned, then called the class back to their seats and handed out a math worksheet. "This is the last task of the day, children, so as soon as you're done, you can have some free time."

Jimmy's head popped up. "Free time? We never get free time. For real?"

"Yes, I said free time."

The kids let out a cheer and dove into their math sheets, hurrying down the list of problems.

"What happened with the board members and Dr. Davis?" Nate asked.

She told him about the events in the parking lot, earning a chuckle from him when she reiterated the line about calling in Ed Spangler. "I'm glad it all worked out in the end," he said.

"Well, we still have a long way to go, but yes, it looks like it will be okay."

"Good."

The sun from the windows reflected off Nate's dark-brown hair. His normally short crew cut had grown out now that he'd been out of the military for a while, as if he, too, were growing into someone else.

She wanted to hope he could have changed from Nate the marine to Nate the ordinary man. In the few days he'd been here, he'd been a different person. And yet, whenever she'd asked him about the future, he'd given her the same answers as he always had: don't count on him because he couldn't predict where he'd be six days or six months down the road.

He could be here tomorrow . . . or gone tomorrow and once again, she'd be left with a heart filled with painful memories.

Jenny realized she'd been wrong about the hot tub. Getting *into* it hadn't been playing with fire. Falling for Nate again had been.

"Well," she said finally, "the best news is that you're all done here." The children were finishing their worksheets, and Jenny collected them as they popped their hands up to indicate they were done. "It's been wonderful having you here this week, Mr. Dole, and we'll miss you when you're gone."

Nate's jaw hardened. Jenny was putting up that wall again, using the class to distance herself. She knew they couldn't discuss anything while the students were around. So she was getting it out of the way now, while he couldn't argue back.

The last student finished her worksheet and Jenny announced the promised free time. In seconds, the class had selected other activities, from drawing to puzzles. Some just moved to other desks and chatted with friends.

Nate grabbed his cane and made his way over to where Jenny sat, on the shelf by the window, looking over the worksheets and marking them with a red pen.

"What if I don't want to leave?" he asked.

She looked up at him, surprise widening her eyes. "There's nothing left to do, Nate. It's the end of the day on Friday. You've done your week, accomplished what you promised. Next week we move on to a new topic."

"And what about you? You move on to a new topic, too?"

The buzz of chatter continued around them, the children caught up in their spontaneous moment of fun. Outside the open windows, cars pulled up in the circular driveway, waiting for dismissal.

"I go back to my life, Nate. Come in to work every day, grade my papers, plan my classes. Nothing new there."

"It sounds sad. Empty."

"It sounds like a job. My job." She dipped her head, back to those damned worksheets again.

He shook his head. "No, it's not. It's a box. You can have a job, but you can have a life, too, Jenny."

A couple of the kids looked up and over at them. "Two minutes, and then it's time to get ready to go home," Jenny told them. That started the chatter up again as the children made good use of their last one hundred and twenty seconds.

But one child didn't. Jimmy picked up the drawing he'd been making and headed over to Nate. "Mr. Dole? I wanted to give this to you."

Nate looked down and saw a crayoned picture of himself and Jimmy, sitting on the rock beneath the tree on the playground. Above them, a bright yellow sun shone in one corner and a few V-shaped birds flew across the rest of the blue expanse of sky. But it was the two figures, composed of simple lines and circles, that got him right in the solar plexus. "Hey, what's this?"

"Nothing." Jimmy drew a circle on the tile floor with his toe. "Just a picture I made."

"It's great, Jimmy. I'm going to hang it on my wall."

"I just wanted to thank you for what you said. I told my mom that story and told her I wanted to make some money of my own, working around the house and stuff."

"Chores, huh? I had a lot of those as a kid."

"Anyway, she and I talked a lot last night and I think things are gonna be better. She's not going to get back together with my dad, but she's going to be home more with me." Jimmy shrugged, as if he didn't care, but Nate could see the happiness in the little boy's eyes. "She said we'll work it out. Whatever that means, but it sounds good to me."

Nate smiled and bent down to Jimmy's level. "I'm glad for you, Jimmy. You're a great kid and you deserve great things."

The boy's face reddened. He mumbled something that sounded like thanks and headed back to his seat.

Nate stared at the picture in his hands. He'd affected a life here, in a way that he'd never affected a life when he'd been in the marines. Sure, he'd defended people, sometimes saved a life, sometimes even taken one if it had been necessary. But never had he ever had such a big return on a simple investment of a few minutes and a few words.

"I told you, they'll get to you," Jenny said quietly. "Before you know it, you'll be collecting retirement from the teachers' fund."

The two-minute warning bell rang and Jenny hopped off the shelf and moved to help the kids get ready to go home. Five minutes later, the classroom was empty and they were alone.

Jenny didn't return to his side. She crossed to her desk and buried herself in her work. She could do a damned good job of dodging him when she wanted to. "Well, thanks again, Nate."

"That's it? Just a thanks? A card in the mail next week, signed by all the kids?" He moved to her desk and laid his hands on either side of it. "Don't avoid me, Jenny. And don't pretend this week didn't happen."

She glanced up, all emotion gone from her eyes, as if she was determined not to betray anything to him. "Let's head this off before anyone gets hurt, Nate. Okay?"

"No, it's not okay. I'm tired of you pushing me away. I'm tired of you telling me you don't want to get involved with me when I know damned well that you do."

He slipped around to her side and turned her chair so she was facing him, unable to hide the war of emotions in her gaze. "Are you telling me you didn't feel a thing when you kissed me?"

"No, I'm not." She pushed back her chair and got to her feet, turning away from him. She trailed her fingers down the chalk board, tracing patterns on the black surface. "Of course I felt something, Nate. I felt *everything*."

"Then why won't you try again, Jenny? I can't leave this room and forget about you. I know better than that now. No matter how hard I tried to forget you over the years, I couldn't. You're a part of me, and I'm a part of you. We've always been that way."

She shook her head. "I can't, Nate."

"Why, damn it?" He let out a gust and circled around so that she had to face him again. "Why?"

She jerked her gaze up to his. "You want to know why I don't like chaos, Nate? Because every week with you was chaos. I couldn't predict anything when I was with you. When you'd be home on leave, when you'd have to go back. Where you'd be. Whether you'd live. I couldn't control any of it." Her eyes misted, then filled with tears. "And most of all, I couldn't control you."

"I didn't mean for it to be that way, Jenny, it's the way the military is. I'm out of that now, though. So there's nothing in our way."

"Yes there is, Nate. It was never the marines that made you that way. It was you." She toyed with the eraser, then let it alone. "You still can't commit to a place, a life, anything. You don't want to put down roots. Why is that?"

"I got Harry. That's a baby step." He tried out a grin, to ease the tension between them, but she didn't give him the answering smile he was hoping for. Behind them, the parking lot emptied, children returning home with their parents, to their families.

"Nate, I don't have time to wait for you to take the big steps. I'm almost thirty. I spent two years of my life getting over you. I'm not going to spend the next sixty years waiting for you to be the kind of man I always wanted."

"I thought I was that man, a long time ago."

She shook her head. "I hate chaos and you hate predictability. We're polar opposites. I'm a third-grade teacher with twenty-five children depending on me to give them an education and a school counting on me to do that and more. You can't tell me you'd be happy sitting in this room — or any room — day after day, living the same life for years on end."

"You don't know that I couldn't."

"And you don't know that you could." Her smile was bittersweet. "I'd say that's an impasse, Nate. The same one we came to nine years ago. This is where I go right and you go left." She picked up her tote bag and slipped it onto her shoulder. "So let's just head off the detour onto Heartbreak Lane now and call it quits before either of us gets in too deep."

As she left the room, Nate realized there was one fatal flaw in Jenny's plan. He was already in too deep — deeper than he'd ever been before.

"Jennifer, have you heard a single word I said?"

Jenny looked up from the dinner plate in front of her to meet her grandfather's eyes. "Uh . . . no. Sorry, Grandpa."

"I was talking about the woman I met while I was walking Spike in the park with the Mercy Dog Club. She was the nicest lady. Shares my love of gardening and even has a little dog, like mine. But it's a dachshund, not a terrier."

"You met a woman at the park with a dachshund?"

"Yep. And we're going to dinner on Saturday night."

Jenny put down her water glass and swallowed her sip before she choked on it. "You have a date?"

He nodded, quite pleased with the event. "Yep. With Alice Marchand."

"With Miss *Marchand?*"

"Don't you remember her? She used to teach you kids back when you were in high school. Biology, I think she said."

"Of course I remember her, Grandpa. This is a small town. You never forget anybody."

Especially the people you cared about the most, the little voice inside her head added. Jenny pushed that thought away. She was here to have dinner with her grandfather, not to dwell on the way things had ended with Nate earlier that afternoon.

"I saw you meet a certain man and his mutt at the park," her grandfather said, interrupting her thoughts. He speared a piece of roast beef onto his fork and ate it before continuing. "Did anything come of that?"

Jenny toyed with her broccoli, merging it with the mashed potatoes and creating more of a mess than a meal. It didn't matter. Her appetite had left her ever since Nate had walked into her classroom and turned her world upside down. "No, nothing."

"You're crazy then."

"Crazy?"

"You're young and you have plenty of years left to enjoy someone. Don't be foolish and set that aside because you think you're doing yourself a favor. You're not."

Leave it to her grandfather to be frank. He was the kind of man who always created a stir at the family reunions because he made it a point to tell the cousins what he really thought about their life choices. "You think I should risk it all?" she asked.

"Of course I do." He pushed his empty plate to the side and crossed his arms in front of him. "You used to be quite the risk taker years ago. Then you got old and safe." He grinned, the wrinkles in his face deepening around the edges of his smile.

"Playing it safe has kept me pretty well thus far in life, Grandpa. I have a house of my own, a retirement fund, a good job —"

"And a lonely heart." He reached across

the table and clasped her hand. "Trust me. None of those things matter one whit at the end of the day when you say 'good night' and there's no one there to echo the words."

"I know." She blinked away the sting in her eyes. When had she turned into this emotional mess?

Easy. When the one man who had always had a finger on the pulse of her heart walked back into her life and turned a perfect layer cake into a jumbled, crying trifle.

Chapter Eleven

★ ★ ★

On Sunday afternoon, Jenny stood outside the white ranch house owned by the Doles and considered leaving. A hundred times over, Jenny had thought twice about the dinner invitation Grace Dole had sent over to her house yesterday. Nate had called and left two messages on her machine, extending the same invitation. Finally, Jenny had relented. She was tired of being afraid of chaos. Afraid that if she let a little in, it would snowball into a lot. And then, before she knew it, her life would end up the same as it had been when she was a child, one topsy-turvy moment after another.

"You made me walk my dog, the least I can do is make you go inside."

Jenny pivoted. "Grandpa! What are you doing here?"

"Same as you, coming to dinner at the Doles. With my date." He grinned and indicated Miss Marchand. She stood beside Jenny's grandfather, in a pink floral dress, and, of all things, a matching pillbox hat. A little flower was pinned over the left side of her chest. "Grace invited us both."

"Miss Marchand! What a nice surprise," Jenny said, trying to keep the shock from her voice. Seeing Alice Marchand with her grandfather was not the picture of romantic bliss she envisioned when she thought of a love story.

"Even an old lady like me can have a little romance in her life, you know." She gave Jenny a wink.

"Where are Spike and Sugarplum?"

Her grandfather took Miss Marchand's hand in his own and gave her a smile. "We left them at home. So we could have a little time to get to know one another without the dogs interrupting."

"Sugarplum gets a little . . . territorial," Miss Marchand explained.

"A little?" Grandpa arched a brow. "My Dockers only have half a leg on one side."

"You exaggerate, Richard. She only got you from the ankle down."

"A small price to pay for your attentions, Alice."

Miss Marchand blushed, the crimson traveling all the way from her cheeks down her neck, turning her nearly the same color as her dress.

So, Miss Marchand wasn't immune to a little love in her own life, too. Well, there was indeed another miracle in the world, right here in the little town of Mercy.

"Are we just going to stand out here, Jennifer, or go on in? And find a little romance for you, too?"

"Grandpa!"

"Well?"

She was outnumbered. Miss Marchand, she half suspected, would drag her in anyway, in her ongoing determination to marry off all the unmarried Doles. Jenny took in a breath, then pressed the doorbell. "Hail, Hail, the Gang's All Here" pealed through the house, inciting the spaniels' barks and a flurry of activity inside.

"Jenny!" Grace Dole flung open the door and immediately greeted her with a smile. "So nice to see you again."

Before she could say a word, she was wrapped up into the Dole family — Jack and Sarah, Katie and Matt, Mark and Claire, Luke and Anita — they all surrounded her as she stepped into the house.

She greeted each in turn, giving Claire, her friend for many years, a strong hug before releasing her. Despite the clamor and the warmth, there was only one face Jenny really cared about seeing.

And then, in the back, away from the group, she saw him. Nate. Standing at the other end of the hall, Harry at his side. Harry let out a little bark of greeting. Nate's face lit up with joy when he caught her eye.

Jenny moved forward, allowing her father and Miss Marchand to take her place in the flurry of greetings. In a dozen steps, she was beside Nate.

"You came."

"Yeah, I did."

"Couldn't resist my mother's cookies? Or me?" He grinned.

"The cookies, of course."

"That's what I figured." He winked. "And what I counted on when my mother conspired with me to invite you."

"Dinner should be on the table in five more minutes, soon as we get these kids corralled," Grace called.

Nate's brothers passed by on their way to the dining room, giving him a few good-natured jabs as they passed. Matt and Katie's twins barreled past next, chasing after one of the dogs, followed by Luke and Anita's toddler, Ben.

"You ready for this chaos?" Nate asked.

"I always liked being with your family. This was the kind of chaos I could understand. With my mother . . . it wasn't predictable. Most days, we were lucky my mother even remembered it was time for dinner. She was always off on some adventure. Sometimes she'd drag me along, and sometimes —"

"She'd forget you."

The hall, which had seemed so busy before, suddenly felt silent, filled with ghosts from her past. "Yeah."

"Just because you live your life with a little spontaneity, Jenny, doesn't make you into that, you know."

She let out a breath. "A big part of me knows that. I mean, I'm a rational adult. But . . ."

"You're not taking any chances, just in case?"

"Basically."

"And I can't change your mind?"

"You, Nate?" She smiled and touched his face for the briefest of seconds. "You are the biggest risk of all."

Grace passed by with a platter of food, reminding them dinner was ready. Jenny slipped away before he could say anything else.

Well, he'd be damned if he was going to let her think loving him was a risk she couldn't afford to take.

Nate didn't know when he'd realized he loved Jenny again. It didn't really matter. He'd never stopped loving her, not really. His feelings had lingered in his heart long after the breakup. He'd carried them with him all these years, from country to country, in and out of battle. She'd been the first thing to pop into his mind when he'd been in a firefight, the one thought that would wake him up in the middle of the night, a deep pang of homesickness crowding into the cot beside him.

When she'd walked into his mother's house today, he'd known. If he'd had any doubts at all, they'd disappeared the second his gaze met her emerald eyes.

He'd always loved Jenny, ever since he'd been born, it seemed. And that was how he wanted it to be for the rest of his life.

Nate took the seat across from Jenny at the dining-room table, watching her talk with Claire and Mark, and set a plan into motion. If there was anything he was good at, it was strategizing.

First item on the plan — to show Jenny once and for all he could be the man she wanted him to be. Gee, glad he'd picked the hardest task first.

His mother came by and gave his

shoulder a squeeze. "Nice to have you at my table again, Nathaniel."

"Nice to be here, Mom."

"How long before you leave again?"

He looked up into Grace Dole's blue eyes and saw sadness there. Had she always looked like that whenever he'd come home? Or had he never taken the time to really look in her eyes and see the toll his military life had taken on the people who loved him?

His father, brothers and sister had fallen silent, listening for his answer. Taking in the faces around him, Nate knew he'd been the stupid one — too wrapped up in rescuing the world to pay attention to what he was doing to everyone else. No more. Those days were over.

"I'm home for good this time," he said.

Stunned silence.

"Forever?" Jack, his oldest brother, said. "Or are you just waiting for new orders?"

"No more orders. No more uniform. Went and got my knee shot up and now I'm taking up space in the unemployment line."

His father leaned back in his chair at the head of the table. "You sure about this, son?"

Nate caught Jenny's gaze from across the

216

way. "As sure as I am that the sun's coming up tomorrow."

She smiled. And that was enough to multiply the hope in his heart ten-fold. Time to introduce a couple of flanking maneuvers.

"So, what are you going to do instead?" his father asked.

"I thought I'd settle down, get married and catch up with the baby-making machine over here." Nate waved at Katie.

"Hey, I take offense to that. Sort of." Katie grinned. "You just have to be smart about it, Nate, and have them two at a time."

"Wait a minute. Am I the only one who just heard Nate say he wants to get married and have kids?" Mark interrupted. He raised his glass of wine. "I say we start offering the toasts now before he changes his mind." Mark, the confirmed bachelor of the family until his marriage last year to a now very pregnant Claire, gave Nate a good-natured wink.

The other Dole men raised their glasses, then swiveled expectant gazes toward Jenny. She sat there, mouth agape, shock clear on her face.

"Uh, Nate, did you ask anyone in particular before you made this announcement?"

Luke asked. "It's not the kind of thing you spring on a girl at a family dinner. Particularly a dinner with *this* family."

Jenny swallowed and wished she had a magical potion to make her disappear. This was not, as Luke had said, the right time or place for life-changing questions.

"I haven't asked Jenny. Yet. But I certainly intend to." Nate's gaze met hers and there was no mistaking the question — or the meaning — in his deep brown eyes.

The fourteen adults squeezed around the Dole dining-room table were as silent as goldfish. At the other end of the room, the five children seated at the card table chattered like magpies, unaware a monumental decision had been laid among the dishes of baked lasagna and garlic bread.

"Luke's right," Jenny said. "This isn't the kind of thing you spring on someone at dinner." She got to her feet, pushing her chair back as she did. She murmured an apology to Grace. "I think I should go."

"Stay," Grace said. "My son has no manners, but the rest of us are pretty civilized."

"Thank you, but . . ." She looked around the table, at the family that had once been as close to her as anyone could be, and shook her head. "I need some time to think."

"I told you that you should have had a ring and flowers," Mark said. "Jeez, Nate, didn't all of us guys getting hitched first teach you anything?"

Jenny left the room, the sound of the Dole men's laughter and gentle ribbing at Nate's inopportune proposal ringing in her ears. She ran for the front door and down the steps. Before she could reach the driveway, Nate was there.

"Wait, Jenny, don't go yet."

She spun around. "Why? Do you have another surprise for me? Something else unexpected? First it's a dip in your brother's hot tub, which, I might add, we got caught doing by his thirteen-year-old daughter. Then it's mice in my classroom, which nearly costs the school its accreditation. Now, you want me to marry you because you threw the proposal out as a joke at the family dinner?"

"It wasn't a joke, Jenny."

"Nate, you've been back in my life for five days. No, six, if you count the ten seconds we spent talking on Sunday. We've been apart for more than nine years. And now, you want me to make a decision about the rest of my life between the salad and the entrée?"

"Yes, I do. Because I know you never

stopped loving me. And I don't want to spend one more day without you."

She turned away, tears hot in her eyes, and shook her head. "Nate, this is the exact kind of crazy thing I avoid. I don't make decisions on the spur of the moment. I don't believe in that *carpe diem* thing. It's a sure way to . . ."

When she didn't finish the sentence, he circled around to the front of her and tipped her chin upward with his finger. "A sure way to what?"

"Get hurt."

"Oh, Jenny," he said, the words so soft, they nearly broke her heart in two, "I'm not going to hurt you. Not anymore."

"How can you guarantee that? You can't. And you know it. I don't take chances, Nate."

"So what are you going to do? Grow old alone, because the only one you think you can count on is yourself?"

"That's my plan. I don't want to be tied down to a man who's going to let me down or hurt me or make my life this crazy, upside-down thing."

"I have news for you, Jenny, you can't count on yourself. Because you are going to change and find out that you aren't who you thought all along."

"What do you mean? I know who I am. I know what I want."

"You want this?" He waved his arm, indicating the quiet, suburban streets behind them. "This predictable life, day in and day out? Dinner at Marge's every Friday? Pizza delivered on Tuesday nights? Bingo at the Presbyterian Church and car washes at the Methodist Church, all as regular as rain in April?"

"Yes, I do."

"Bull."

She swallowed. "How can you say that to me? You haven't seen me in nine years. You don't know what I want now."

"I know *you,* Jenny. I know you better than anyone in the entire world."

She looked into his eyes and knew that was true. She'd never opened up to anyone as much as she had in those years with Nate. Her mother had been too flighty to know her only child, her father had been at work more often than he was home. Even her closest friends believed her to be Jenny Wright, prim and proper third-grade teacher. No one had seen the same Jenny that Nate had.

"You know who you *thought* I was."

"What, did you get a personality transplant? Because the girl I knew wanted to do more than just live in this little town. She wanted to travel the world and see the sights. Write about them in essays that she planned to send out to magazines someday." Nate ran a thumb under her eye, wiping away a tear trailing down her cheek. His voice softened. "She wanted more. Much more. What happened to her?"

"She grew up. Got a job. Responsibilities."

"And had her heart broken by a stupid marine who didn't appreciate what he had."

A second tear escaped and slid down her face. Thick, pent-up emotion clogged her throat. All over again, the ache in her heart throbbed, as if it had happened today, not a decade ago. "Yeah," she said softly.

"Let me tell you about that marine." Again, he caught the tear with a finger and whisked it away. "I didn't join the military because I wanted to save the world. I joined because I was scared."

"You? You aren't scared of anything."

"Sure I am. Remember me as a kid? I didn't have the brains of Luke or the athletic ability of Mark. Jack always knew he wanted to be a cop from the day he was born, and Katie, well, she had the energy to be anything. I was . . . the runt of the litter, even though I wasn't the youngest. I wasn't big and strong in school and I got lucky when Ricky Lincoln made friends with me because it sure protected my butt from the bullies."

"You sure grew up to be . . ." Her gaze drifted over his muscular frame, the defined shoulders, tapered waist. "Imposing."

"Nothing a good weight bench and a lot of determination couldn't do. I became a marine because it made me feel invincible. Strong enough to take on the world and especially the bad guys. Then, when I couldn't be a marine anymore, I felt like that kid all over again. Weak, worth nothing more than a piece of paper."

"Oh, Nate, that's not you. You know that, don't you?"

"I do now." He took her hands, strong wide palms holding her smaller ones with security and honesty. "When Jimmy gave me that drawing, I saw that I didn't have to have my uniform on to make a difference. Being a marine didn't make me a man and it didn't make me strong. It sounds corny, but I realized all I had to do was be me."

"Corny isn't bad, you know. It fits right in with Mercy."

He chuckled. "That it does."

In unspoken communication, they traversed the driveway and stepped onto the lawn. Soft blades of dark-green growth sprouted anew from the earth. "But why . . . why did you distance yourself from everyone when you were in the military? It was like the longer you were there, the less you let anyone into your heart."

"Because if there's one thing the military teaches you, it's that people die. And die young. I saw my friends die on the battlefield and learned pretty damned quick that getting close to people did nothing but make me vulnerable, and that's the last thing you want to be when you're fighting an enemy. So I distanced myself, from the men I was with . . . and the people I loved."

They crossed to an oval concrete bench under an oak tree and took a seat in the shade. A robin hopped down from the tree and picked at the grass, searching for a late-day worm.

"Then I got shot. At first, I felt sorry for myself. All I could think about was how this had ruined my career. Once I got over the pity party, I realized how close I came to dying. A couple of feet higher, and that bullet would have been in my heart, not my kneecap."

Jenny closed her eyes and shuddered. She couldn't imagine losing Nate like that. For just a second, the thought of a flag-draped casket coming back to Mercy instead of him rocketed through her. All the time they'd dated, it had been her worst nightmare. To think of how close he'd come to that scared her, even now. "I'm glad the shooter had bad aim."

"Me, too." He smiled. "Now I realize, though, how stupid it was to keep my distance from the people I love. And to keep thinking that not putting down roots would keep me from getting too attached. Well, I have news for you, Jenny. I want to get attached. I want roots. I want *you*." He took her hand, his thumb circling the back. "I could die tomorrow or, you could be stuck with me for sixty more years. Either way, I don't want to let five more minutes go by without telling you how I feel. I won't let you go again, Jenny, and live those sixty years alone and full of regret."

She got to her feet and ran a hand through her hair. "That's what you say today, Nate. How can I know you'll mean it tomorrow?"

He rose to stand behind her and wrapped his arms around her waist. "Sometimes, Jenny, you have to take a leap of faith and know there's someone you love waiting at the bottom to catch you."

"It's a pretty big leap you're asking of me."

"Be adventurous," he whispered, his breath warm against her ear, awakening every nerve in her body, "and love me as much as I love you."

She pivoted to face him. For a long time, Jenny studied his face. In her gut, she heard the answer she'd been seeking. Just as Nate had promised Jimmy, all the answers were already there. Joy that she'd finally found what she'd been seeking, and that she'd allowed herself to trust in it, ran through her. "Only if you promise me one thing."

"Name it."

"There won't be any llamas at our wedding." Then she leaned forward and kissed him, before the look of surprise could disappear from his eyes.

Epilogue

★ ★ ★

"I can't believe I let you talk me into this," Jenny shouted over the roar of the engines. "I must be crazy."

"Crazy in love." Nate grinned, then leaned over and checked the straps across Jenny's chest. Confident they were secure, he turned to his own and did a double-check there, too. "You said you wanted a little more spontaneity in your life."

"A little. Not a sky-full."

He just grinned more at her. "Wait till you see what I have planned for our honeymoon, baby."

A surge of excitement and fear ran through Jenny. She adjusted her veil, made sure her dress was secure, then took her husband-to-be's hand and stepped forward on the platform. "You know our students will never stop talking about this."

"If they ever pause long enough from naming all those mouse babies." Nate had been hired as a permanent aide in her class while he went back to school to get his teaching degree. Dr. Davis had been thrilled with the improvement in the school and the boost in the state test scores at the end of the school year, which had assured Mercy Elementary's accreditation.

"At least we caught those last two mice finally."

"Unfortunately, after they had a little fun in the back of the classroom."

Jenny laughed. It had taken three weeks to find the last two strays, long enough for them to start making themselves at home — and then some. "Good thing it's only third grade. I didn't have to give too many details on where that nest of babies came from."

"Give it time, Jenny, and you'll be explaining more than just that. At least, that's my plan." He gave her another grin, then put a palm over her flat stomach. "Let's see what we can cook up on our honeymoon."

The thought of a baby — her and Nate's baby — soared through her. Claire and Mark had welcomed a daughter into the world last month. Miss Marchand, who'd been a regular visitor to Jenny's grandfather's house, had started dropping hints lately about the last Dole son's failure to procreate. Yet.

If Jenny had anything to do with it, it wouldn't be long before there'd be another nursery to decorate. Nate's live-for-the-moment advice had started to rub off on her — and her biological clock — ever since they'd set a wedding date.

"Have I told you lately that I love you, even though I think you're insane?" she said, smiling at him.

"Long as you marry me right now, that's all I care about."

The minister behind them cleared his throat. Jenny and Nate pivoted, hands clasped, and in a few minutes, had recited the words that joined them for life, for better or worse.

"Ready?" Nate asked her.

"As ready as I'll ever be." She did a 180-degree turn with Nate by her side and faced the roaring sky going by. The farms of the outlying areas of Mercy, more than twelve thousand feet below them, looked like a jigsaw puzzle full of rectangles. A multicolored bouquet of balloons and wedding guests stood beneath a huge "Congratulations" sign and a great big X to mark the spot where the new Mr. and Mrs. Dole were to make their landing.

"Okay, here we go. One. Two. Three!"

Nate clutched Jenny's hand and together the two of them leaped off the side of a perfectly good airplane and into the air, spiraling down fast and furious.

She should have been terrified. But with Nate's hand holding hers — and a damned good parachute on her back — Jenny felt more secure than she ever had in her life.

About the Author

★ ★ ★

Shirley Jump spends her days writing romantic comedies with sweet attitude to feed her shoe addiction and avoid housework. A wife and mother of two, her real life helps her maintain her sense of humor. She swears that if she didn't laugh, she'd be fatally overcome by things like uncooperative llamas at birthday parties and chipmunks in the bathroom. When she isn't writing, Shirley's either eating or shopping. Or on a really good day, doing both at the same time.

He first novel for Silhouette, *The Virgin's Proposal*, won the Bookseller's Best Award in 2004. Though she framed the award, it didn't impress the kids enough to make them do the dishes more often. In fact, life as a published author is pretty much like life as it was before, except now Shirley conveniently pulls a deadline out of thin air whenever laundry piles up.

Read excerpts, see reviews or learn more about Shirley at www.shirleyjump.com.

We hope you have enjoyed this Large Print book. Other Thorndike, Wheeler or Chivers Press Large Print books are available at your library or directly from the publishers.

For more information about current and upcoming titles, please call or write, without obligation, to:

Publisher
Thorndike Press
295 Kennedy Memorial Drive
Waterville, ME   04901
Tel. (800) 223-1244

Or visit our Web site at:
www.gale.com/thorndike
www.gale.com/wheeler

OR

Chivers Large Print
published by BBC Audiobooks Ltd
St James House, The Square
Lower Bristol Road
Bath BA2 3BH
England
Tel. +44(0) 800 136919
email: bbcaudiobooks@bbc.co.uk
www.bbcaudiobooks.co.uk

All our Large Print titles are designed for easy reading, and all our books are made to last.